30
SUGAR CREEK GANG
The BLUE COW

Paul Hutchens

MOODY PRESS
CHICAGO

2516

PREFACE

Hi—from a member of the Sugar Creek Gang!

It's just that I don't know which one I am. When I was good, I was Little Jim. When I did bad things—well, sometimes I was Bill Collins or even mischievous Poetry.

You see, I am the daughter of Paul Hutchens, and I spent many an hour listening to him read his manuscript as far as he had written it that particular day. I went along to the north woods of Minnesota, to Colorado, and to the various other places he would go to find something different for the Gang to do.

Now the years have passed—more than fifty, actually. My father is in heaven, but the Gang goes on. All thirty-six books are still in print and now are being updated for today's readers with input from my five children, who also span the decades from the '50s to the '70s.

The real Sugar Creek is in Indiana, and my father and his six brothers were the original Gang. But the idea of the books and their ministry were and are the Lord's. It is He who keeps the Gang going.

PAULINE HUTCHENS WILSON

1

I'd been hoping and hoping all through that long, slow winter that when spring came the gang could happen onto a new kind of adventure, one in which I myself, red-haired, more-or-less-fiery-tempered Bill Collins, would get a chance to use my muscles and my presence of mind to save myself or somebody from danger.

It's not that there generally wasn't plenty of excitement around Sugar Creek, especially when the gang was together. We were able to stumble onto more topsy-turvy, hair-raising adventures than you could shake a stick at. But—well, who wants to have such ordinary experiences as getting his nose bashed in a fierce, fast fistfight? Or taking a wet pet lamb to school on a rainy, muddy day to see if it really *would* make the children laugh and play? Or killing an ordinary black bear at the bottom of Bumblebee Hill?

Besides, it was Little Jim, the littlest member of the Sugar Creek Gang, who had killed the mad old mother bear, and he had done it with Big Jim's rifle, which he accidentally had at the time. All I had gotten to do in that tense excitement, while Little Jim was being the hero, was to watch and cringe, feel scared half to death, scream, and a few other things any ordinary boy could have done.

What I really wanted to do sometime was to kill a bear myself, take a picture of it, and then have it mounted—or maybe have it made into a rug for our living-room floor like the one Old Man Paddler has on the floor of his old clapboard-roofed cabin in the Sugar Creek hills. He had killed it himself, as a boy, with an old-fashioned muzzle-loading gun.

"So you want to kill a bear yourself, do you?" Dad asked me one sunshiny spring day when there was a lot of farmwork to do and I couldn't even go fishing. We were sitting at our kitchen table at the time, eating lunch. Mom was at her place at the side of the table nearest the stove, and Dad was near the water pail behind him and also near both doors, one of which I would have to use if I wanted to go outdoors in a hurry to get in a little play before the afternoon's work would start.

I was sitting on the long wooden bench opposite Mom and against the south wall of the kitchen, and Charlotte Ann, my mischievous, cute little sister, was in her high chair between Mom and Dad, wiggling and squirming and eating with the best toddler table manners I ever saw.

"Yes sir," I replied in answer to Dad's question, making my answer short because I was at the same time trying to make short work of a piece of Mom's cherry pie. She had baked it that very morning, since most mothers hadn't anything exciting to do to get their pictures in the paper. They only did such ordinary things as ironing and washing and patching a boy's and his father's clothes and cooking their food and keeping the house clean seven days a week and, in the summertime, making garden and setting hens and stuff like that.

And Dad said, not realizing how I felt at the time, "You wouldn't settle for some ordinary wild animal such as a wildcat or a timber wolf or even a moose?"

"Kids' stuff!" I said and frowned down into my plate, knowing that if I had had a mirror and had been looking into it, I would have seen not only my reddish hair and freckles and a pair of reddish brown eyebrows like my father's, but there would be a wrinkle in my forehead like the kind our leader, Big Jim, had when he frowned about something. And if I had looked close enough, I could actually have seen what, if it kept on growing, might become a mustache on my upper lip.

"How old are you now?" Dad asked.

Before I could answer, Mom answered, "The question is wrong. It should be, 'How *young* are you?'"

And then I *knew* there would have been a Big Jim frown on my forehead, because if there is anything a boy doesn't like more than he doesn't like anything else, it's for somebody—especially one of his parents—to remind him he is as young as he is.

"I'm just a child," I said, having that very minute made the last of the short work I was making out of her pie, "probably too young to

7

help with the dishes today—if I may be excused." I slid out of my place on the long bench as easily as pie, saying at the same time, "I'll be down at the barn if you need me for anything."

Dad's long arm, with a strong, calloused left hand on the end of it, stopped me by the overall suspenders before I could get to my feet and my feet could get me to the door. His voice helped a little as he said, "Not so fast, sir."

"I can do it slowly," I said. I stayed stopped, shutting my right eye and trying to push my upper lip out far enough to see it by looking straight down the left side of my nose.

"Should you make such a face?" Mom asked. It seemed from the tone of voice she had used that she was glad Dad had stopped me.

Because Dad and Mom and I liked each other extrawell most of the time, and were always trying to be funny to each other, and sometimes not being very, I said, "I didn't make it—I inherited it."

Mom was really quick on the trigger then. She tossed in a bright remark: "Poor boy! Your father shouldn't be blamed too much, though. He inherited his own red hair and complexion from *his* parents."

I felt myself grinning. "You're cute parents, but personally I think I look like a meadowlark's egg with a face on it which somebody tried to draw and didn't quite finish."

I was remembering a nestful of eggs I'd

seen once right after a mother meadowlark had exploded off it while I was running through the south pasture. Each egg was white with a lot of reddish brown freckles all over it.

It was Poetry, my barrel-shaped friend, who had given me the face idea. He had once said to me when he had been trying to count the freckles I had on only one side of my face, "You look like a meadowlark's egg with a half-finished face drawn on it by a boy who gets poor grades in art in school."

Dad was still holding onto my suspenders, and I didn't dare to go on outdoors for fear he would be left holding an empty pair of overalls at the kitchen table. He said, "I believe you're right, son. Now you can run along to the barn. You might like to get the posthole digger, take it up to the pignut trees, and run that corner posthole down another fifteen or so inches. We'll have to get the fence up as soon as we can —or even sooner. You know how Jersey Jill likes new clover—and how dangerous it is when she eats too much."

"Yes sir," I said, glad to dig postholes or most anything that I could use my muscles on rather than do something around the house. Whoever heard of a boy developing strong muscles or even growing a mustache faster by carrying a dish towel around somebody's kitchen?

On the way to the barn I stopped at the iron pitcher pump for a drink, skinned the cat twice at the grape arbor, and chinned myself eight times to strengthen my biceps. Then I went on out to the barn, stopping twice more on the way.

One time was to speak to Old Addie, our red mother hog, who was grunting around the gate as if she wished she could have breakfast, dinner, and supper fifty times a day. Addie lived in a new apartment hog house over on the farther side of her pen, where nearly every spring she gave the Collins family seven or eight nice little red-haired piglets.

"Good afternoon," I said down to her. But she only grunted a disgusted reply as though it was still too early in the day to talk to anybody and she hadn't had her cup of coffee yet.

"Such a face," I said to her. "Should you be making such a face?"

And do you know what? She grunted out a nasal sort of answer that sounded like: "I didn't make it. I just inherited it." And because I had said it first in the kitchen as Dad was holding onto my overall suspenders, it sounded kind of funny.

The second time I stopped was when I reached the hole just below the north window of the barn, where Mixy, our black-and-white cat, goes in and out a hundred times a day and which she uses for a refuge when some neighbor's dog is chasing her. She must have heard me talking to Old Addie, because she came out stretching and yawning as if she had just awakened from a nap. Then she made a beeline for my overall legs. As I stood looking down at her, she arched her back and rubbed herself past me two or three times.

"You're a nice cat," I said down to her. There was something nice about having old Mixy do that to me, making it seem she liked me a lot—and anybody likes to be liked, better than anything else.

Pretty soon I had the posthole digger out of the place where Dad kept it in the corner by the cabinet where he keeps his different stock medicines and tools and things for working around the barn.

Just as I reached for the digger, which was standing beside a shovel, I noticed that Dad had added a new book to his little farm library. He was always adding a book every now and then, anyway. This one was called *A Veterinary Handbook for the Average Farmer, or What to Do Before the Doctor Arrives.*

The big book was standing on the shelf beside a dozen others with long names such as *Farm Work Simplification* and *Soil Microbiology* and a few with ordinary titles such as *Vegetable Gardening, All About Field Crop Insects,* and one that sounded as if it ought to be on the shelf in our kitchen. That one was *How to Feed a Hungry Man.*

I quick leafed through the new book, just to see what Dad had been studying.

Sometimes when we were working together in the garden or in the cornfield, he would start to explain something to me, and I always liked to say, "Sure, that's right. Now you can go to the head of the class." And then, before he could start to tell me anything else, I would tell him first and try to ask questions he couldn't answer, so that I could say, "Sorry, Theodore," calling him by his first name as if I was a teacher in our red-brick schoolhouse and he a boy in maybe the fifth grade.

It took me only what seemed six minutes to read a half chapter on what to do if your cow or calf gets what is called "bloat," which was where Dad had left a bookmark and maybe was where he had been reading last.

Then I quickly took up the posthole digger. It was the hinged type with long steel blades that could take a big ten-inch bite of dirt in its six-inch-diameter jaws. A man or boy using its five-foot-long handles could dig a fast hole most anywhere on the Theodore Collins farm.

Then I was out the barn door, stepping all around and over Mixy to keep her from getting smashed under my feet. And in a minute I was up by the pignut trees, working and sweating and feeling fine, with my powerful biceps lifting big bites of yellowish clay out of the posthole and piling them onto a yellow brown mound beside me.

Several blackbirds, thinking maybe I'd unearth a grub or a night crawler or something, came flying and walking around excitedly. But I wasn't interested—not much, anyway, until I happened to think what they were there for. For some reason that made me think what else night crawlers were good for, and all of a sudden I remembered I hadn't gone fishing for almost two days. And the sun was shining down so warm and getting warmer every minute. In fact, it was getting *hotter* every minute. It would be a shame not to go fishing.

I hardly realized what happened after that, but in almost no time I had left the posthole digger down in the hole with a big bite of yellow clay in its jaws. I had gone to the barn and come back with the shovel and was over by the garden fence, not far from a pile of boards, digging up some of the nicest fishing worms that ever tempted a sunfish and was putting them into a tin can I found close by. The reason I hardly realized what I was doing was that in my mind I was already down at the mouth of the branch, where Poetry, my barrel-shaped friend, and I nearly always could catch quite a few fish.

I soon found out what I was doing, though, because suddenly out of nowhere there was a voice behind me saying, "I didn't want the posthole dug *there,* Son—over *here* where the fence is to go up. And you can't dig a posthole scratching around on the surface with a shovel!"

I felt my face turn as red as my hair, and with quick presence of mind I said, "Take a look in the hole over there. See if I haven't dug it deep enough. No use to dig it too deep and have to fill it up."

Dad picked up a clod of dirt and tossed it at several blackbirds, not because he didn't like them but because he was still a little like a boy that had to throw something at something every time he saw something to throw something at.

Then he took a squint down into the hole my biceps had made and, taking the digger by its long ash handles, brought up a big yellow bite of clay and emptied it onto the top of the mound beside the hole. He absolutely surprised me by saying, "If you can wait till the bass season opens, I'll take two days off, and we'll run up to Little Wolf and catch some big ones. We really ought to get the fence up first, though, don't you think?"

It was hard to believe my ears, and it was also hard not to get to go down to the mouth of the branch right that very minute. But I knew Dad was right. I gave up and helped him finish setting the big corner post, but not till I had tried another idea that came to my mind, which was: "That's a long time to ask Mom to wait for a fish supper, when she likes sunfish and goggle-eyes just as much as she does bass. She could have fish for supper tonight if anybody would just say the word."

But Dad wouldn't say the word. And I could tell by the way I felt that it wouldn't be a good idea for me to say even one more word about it. So I started in strengthening my biceps again, using the posthole digger, while Dad got busy with a saw and hammer and nails, making a crossbar on the bottom end of the big cedar post we were going to set in the hole.

As soon as we had the hole finished and the crossbar on the post, we carefully eased the heavy post in, piling big rocks onto the cross-bar in the bottom of the hole and tamping gravel and hard clay all around the rocks. Finally we filled the hole all the way to the top, tamping it hard all the way.

It took us nearly all afternoon to get it all done, but it was fun. And Dad learned quite a few things he pretended he didn't know before about what to do before the doctor comes in case old Jersey Jill, our fawn-colored milk cow, ate too much dew-wet clover some morning on an empty stomach, and gas built up in her paunch, and she couldn't belch, and the gas got worse and worse, and she swelled up more and more, and her left flank bulged so badly it looked as if she was twice as big as she ought to be.

"That," Dad said after I'd told him, "is what to do *after* you've called the vet and while you're waiting for him to come, or if he can't come right away."

But it wasn't only fun. That information about cows was also something every farmer ought to know, because he could lose an expensive cow or heifer in just thirty minutes after she started to get the bloat, if something wasn't done to save her.

"But *this* that we're doing right now is what to do so you won't *have* to call the veterinarian," Dad explained. "A good fence will keep your cattle out until you're ready to let them in. And never, *never* let a hungry cow loose in a field of white clover or alfalfa or ladino clover or even crimson clover when the dew is on it, or in any pasture with a high percentage of legumes. The very minute you see your cow or sheep beginning to bloat, get after her; make her keep moving, chase her up a hill—anything to make her belch."

"Right," I said to Dad. "You can go to the head of the class."

"You go," Dad said with a joke in his voice. "I've been there so often and stayed so long at a time that it would be nice for the rest of the class to have a chance."

I had the handle of the fence-stretcher in my hands at the time, strengthening my biceps by pulling on it and stretching the fence at the same time. I was wondering—if I had my shirt off—if anybody could see the muscles of my back working like big ropes under the skin as I'd seen Big Jim's do.

I answered Dad by saying, "I'm not so much interested in going to the head of the class as I am to the mouth of the branch."

I didn't look up when I said it but kept on making steady, rhythmic movements and feeling fine, not expecting my remark to do more than make Dad grunt like Old Addie and make a face like the kind a father shouldn't have to make too many times in one day.

He stopped all of a sudden, looked at his watch to see what time it was, and then at the sun in the west to see if his watch was right. He said, "If you think the night crawlers might be a little crowded in that small can, you could empty a few of them out one at a time down where the branch empties into the creek. If you hurry, you can get back with enough sunfish for supper."

Suddenly my biceps felt as strong as they needed to, and I looked into Dad's gray green eyes under his shaggy brows to see if he meant it, and he honest-to-goodness did. Just to be sure, though, I said, "Shouldn't I gather the eggs first? Or help feed the horses and chickens and carry in another load of wood for Mom?"

"Orders are orders," Dad said. "I'm testing your obedience. Go on and go fishing."

I looked at my own watch and saw it was still only four o'clock. I'd have at least one hour to sit on the bank in the shade of the sycamores and watch my bobber run around in little circles and plop under. I'd have an hour to see the dragonflies flitting around, and listen to frogs piping and birds singing, and smell the nice, fresh spring weather that for several weeks had been making the whole county the most wonderful place in the world to be alive in.

"My mother has taught me always to obey my father," I said.

It wasn't more than three minutes before I was started on the way to my favorite sport, my cane fishing pole in one hand and the can of worms in the other, running a barefoot-boy race toward the house, where I had to phone Poetry to see if he could go with me.

I stormed into the house and was on our

party-line phone before Mom, who was upstairs doing something or other, realized what was going on.

Poetry's mother answered, and I quickly asked if I could talk to Poetry. It was very important, I told her.

"Sorry," she said, "but he's down at the creek somewhere. He's trying to catch a few fish for our supper."

"Thank you very much," I said politely and hung up quick.

Then I was outdoors and racing through the orchard toward Poetry's dad's woods and the mouth of the little branch that winds a sunshiny way through it to the place where it empties into Sugar Creek and where the sunfish always are, if there are any.

I might even run into some kind of exciting adventure before I get back, I thought as I flew along. When you are with mischievous, detective-minded Poetry, you never can tell when your innocent fun is going to turn into a hair-raising experience of some kind, as it has done quite a few times in my life.

Over the last fence and through the woods I went, feeling as fine as anything, better even than the way a certain poet whose poem we had had to memorize in school felt when he wrote, "I know a place where the sun is like gold, and the cherry blooms burst with snow, and down underneath is the loveliest nook where the four-leaf clovers grow."

I was smelling the sweet smell of wild plum

blossoms right that minute, and the sun glinting on the water of the riffle of the branch toward which I was racing was like live silver hurrying on its way to the creek. Poetry and I wouldn't need any four-leaf clovers to help us have good luck. I was sure of it as I dashed down the hill on one of about thirty-seven paths made by boys' bare feet that crossed and crisscrossed the countryside everywhere.

It certainly felt fine to be free from work for a while. But I never dreamed that, while Poetry and I were in the middle of some of the best luck we had ever had, we'd be interrupted by one of the most nonsensical experiences.

I didn't have any idea, either, that before sundown that day I'd get my temper all stirred up by the beginning of a series of adventures that would be different from any we had ever had—and that, before the summer was half through, I'd really need some of the information I had read in Dad's new book, which he had on the shelf of the tool cabinet by the north window of our barn, named *What to Do Before the Doctor Arrives*.

2

Poetry was at the mouth of the branch before I was, and he already had almost three fish. He was sitting on a root at the base of a big sycamore tree with his cane pole in both hands, his face tense, and his eyes focused on his line, which was hanging loose on the end of his pole about fifteen feet out in the lazy water.

He hardly looked at me when I showed up in the path that runs from the little bridge to the mouth of the branch. He just half glanced back over his shoulder, scowled, and shook his head, meaning to keep still as he might be getting a bite.

"You caught any?" I whispered.

He whispered back, *"Sh!"* holding up three fingers to show me how many.

I looked down at the edge of the water to see if he had a stringer there and to see what kind he had. But I couldn't see a single fish. The stringer was still coiled up beside him on the ground.

As quickly and as quietly as I could, except for breathing hard from running, I baited my hook as I whispered, looking at the empty stringer, "I thought you said you had *three*."

"Not three," he answered. "Just *almost* three."

My line was out right away, and my red-and-white bobber was in the middle of a small circle of widening waves it had just made when it landed not more than five feet from Poetry's bottle-cork bobber. On the hook on the end of my line were six long fishing worms, each of them dangling. I knew if they were doing what ordinary fishing worms do on a hook, they were down there near the bottom of the creek, twisting and squirming and wrapping themselves around the shank of the hook like the arms and legs of six boys on the ground in one tangled-up pile in a football game.

Saying "almost three" was silly, and I said so to Poetry, who answered with another shush, adding, "Just as soon as I get this one and two more, I'll have *three*."

It was supposed to be a joke, so Poetry laughed. Then he stopped quick as his bobber started moving around in a circle, then dived under and stayed under. His line went tight, and *wham!* Poetry set the hook, and I could see he really had something.

Wham again out there! And this time it was *my* line. My bright red-and-white bobber made a plunking noise as it smacked the water and shot under just as my line went tight. The two of us let out yells, each of us saying, "I've got a fish!"

And we had. *Really* had, I mean. I had never felt such a heavy weight on my line in Sugar Creek. Why, this fish felt as if it was as big as one of Old Addie's piglets, and it kept running wild down under the water, making me actually need all the strength of my powerful biceps as I held on for dear life.

"Get your line out of my way," Poetry ordered, "or we'll get them crossed and lose both of them!"

Because he was right next to the branch, I knew he couldn't go more than four feet in his direction without having to get into hip-deep water and getting all wet. But I could go left down the creek and probably land my fish there.

So I worked my way along the slippery bank as fast as I could, without stumbling and without letting that monster fish of some kind get a slack line. In a few seconds I was the whole length of a cane pole from where Poetry, on his bare feet, was struggling to land his own fish.

Neither of us had reels on our poles, but we were trying to do what you generally do with a fish when you have just a cane pole and only a line.

"I'm getting mine!" Poetry cried happily. "He's coming!"

"So am I!" I cried back.

A second later a great big yellow-stomached, brown-backed, bullhead fish, a foot long and with horns on his head, came struggling up through the excited water, battling against my biceps and stirring up a lot of new waves and foam. If any other fish had been around, they'd have been scared half to death.

And then I got a sickening surprise as Poetry shouted, "Hey, you! You've got your line wrapped around mine!"

What a letdown! I was disgusted. "It's your fault!" I cried to my best friend. "If your old fish hadn't made a beeline for mine, he wouldn't have gotten all tangled up in it."

Well, there wasn't anything I could do but help Poetry pull in his fish. In another minute, I thought, we'd land him together, and then it'd be fifteen minutes of wasted time while we untangled our lines before we could start fishing again.

And all for a silly bullhead or catfish. It was probably a catfish, which is in the same family as a bullhead, anyway. At least I, Bill Collins, hadn't wasted my perfectly wonderful, juicy-tasting six-wormed bait on a slimy bullpout. That is another name for the dumbest-looking kind of fish that lives in Sugar Creek.

In another minute, sure enough, we had landed it, and it *was* a whopper! Boy oh boy! We swung him away back up onto the bank about fifteen feet from the water's edge and into the tall weeds and bushes behind us. And then both of us went back to see how big he really was and to get our lines untangled.

Talk about a surprise! What to my wondering eyes should appear but—

"Hey!" I cried excitedly. "He's on *my* hook! He's *my* fish! It was your dumb old line that got tangled up and wrapped itself around *mine!*"

"It was not! He's on my hook!" my best friend thundered back at me. "It's your dumb old line that—"

Poetry stopped short of finishing what he

23

had started to say and exclaimed, "Well, for land's sake. *Look,* would you!"

I had already seen. That giant-headed bull-head or catfish had *both* hooks in his huge mouth, and his beady black eyes were glaring at us as much as to say, "It's *both* your faults! You *tricked* me!"

And we were both right. We had both caught a fish, maybe the biggest one there ever was in Sugar Creek. Boy oh boy! Our lines were entangled plenty, but nobody was to blame.

That is, I thought nobody was, but Poetry for some reason was stubborn about it. "My bobber went under first! He took my bait first!"

I looked at the huge mouth and remembered how hard it was to clean a bullhead. In a second I had my knife out of my pocket and had cut off my line right where it entered the cavernous mouth, saying cheerfully, "OK, pal, he struck your line first. He's your fish. I'll see if I can catch another. You untangle the lines while I get started."

I quickly snipped off the other end of my line at the end of the pole where I had it tied and in a jiffy was on my way out of the bushes, hurrying toward the creek and taking another line out of my pocket as I went. *Let him be selfish,* I thought. *Let him have his old fish. Let him untangle the lines himself.*

And right then is where we ran into something else we had to untangle, and it took both of us to do it.

Like the sound of a hippopotamus running

or something as big, a noise sounded in the bushes and tall weeds behind us. *Smashety-crashety-swishety*.

What on earth! It was coming straight toward us, and I could imagine it to be as big as a circus elephant—and as dangerous, if you happened to be in the way while it was charging toward you!

"Look out!" Poetry yelled behind me. "Get out of the way, or you'll get crushed under her feet!"

I looked out, and I jumped out of the way of something as long and as tall and as wide as I had always imagined a rhinoceros would be if it was like the ones I'd seen in the animal picture book I had in my library in my upstairs room.

And its color was *blue!* Blue, imagine! And it had horns and wild eyes and was crashing through the underbrush as if there wasn't any there.

Poetry was on the ground by the catfish or bullhead, whichever it was, and was all tangled up in the lines. And all I had to defend him with—because he couldn't get up—was my lineless cane pole. I quickly whirled around and started yelling in the direction of the horned wild animal. I rushed toward it and screamed for it to stop.

If it didn't stop, it would charge feetfirst through the underbrush into the little tangle of weeds and shrubs where Poetry, my best friend, was down and couldn't get untangled in time to save himself.

It was a tense minute, and it didn't make any difference whose fishing worms had caught whose fish. I *had* to save Poetry. I still had my straw hat on, and I started waving it as I yelled.

And then the animal stopped and stood stock-still. I saw its face as clearly as anything. What I was seeing didn't seem possible, but I was seeing it, anyway. It was a wild-eyed, scared cow. A skinny, half-starved-looking *blue* cow!

She saw me at the same time I saw her, and she was probably as surprised at seeing a boy with red hair on the top of his head as I was in seeing a blue-haired cow. She whirled, snorted, raised her tail up over her back, swerved to the right, and charged toward the branch, not stopping till she had landed out in the middle of it in water up to her stomach.

And then I saw a very round boy with a long stick in one hand, puffing down the incline near the bridge and hurrying toward us. Seeing me, he started yelling, "You leave my cow alone! Don't you dare hit her with that old fish."

And then I knew who it was.

I cried out to Poetry, "It's Shorty Long!"

He was the new boy who had moved into our neighborhood one winter and who had caused a whole lot of trouble for our gang. But then his folks had moved again, and we hadn't heard from him since.

What was *he* doing in our territory again? Had his folks moved back? I certainly hoped not. He had almost divided our gang by getting

Dragonfly, our pop-eyed member, on his side and teaching him some filthy-minded things a decent boy doesn't care to know.

Imagine that! Shorty was the only person in the world who was as hard to get along with as my city cousin, Wally Sensenbrenner, who had been to visit us with his nonsensical copper-colored dog and had upset the whole neighborhood. Shorty was just as bad, or worse, and he had brought with *him* a blue cow! *Blue,* mind you! It didn't make sense!

Also, I could tell from just one look at that wild-eyed quadruped that she wouldn't have any respect for boundaries of any kind. And most any farmer in the Sugar Creek territory could expect to wake any morning, or maybe any midnight, and find her in his cornfield or pasture or orchard or strawberry patch. If she didn't know any more than to come charging into the privacy of a boy's favorite fishing place and then, when she got stopped, to plunge horns first out into the branch—

But I didn't have time to do any more worrying about what she might do in the future, because right that second Shorty was after her, trying to round her up so that he could get her back to the road.

And a second later, she started on a wild, splashing run up the middle of the branch toward the bridge.

"Crazy old dumb bunny!" Shorty's squawky voice cried after her and also toward us, maybe to get our sympathy. "She absolutely refuses to cross that bridge! She's scared to death of it. And I've got to get her home. You guys come help me!"

"Where's home?" I called to him.

He called back, "First house past Dragon-fly's."

In the next few fast-flying seconds, I was remembering the first time I had met Shorty Long. It was in the wintertime, and he had accidentally run face first into a snowball I had made and thrown with all my might toward the corner of our barn. I didn't know he was going to come around the corner just in time to get squished with it.

There had been a rough-and-tumble fight in a snowdrift right after that, till we had gotten well enough acquainted to stop fighting, which I was glad to do. I had just had the wind knocked out of me and was struggling to get out of that snowdrift I had plunged headfirst into.

While I was gasping for breath because of having had the wind knocked out of me and from being smothered in the snowdrift, Mom had come out the back door of our house just in time to invite all of us in to have a piece of blackberry pie, which she had just that minute taken out of the oven.

Well, a boy in trouble is a boy in trouble, so it seemed I ought to try to help Shorty. I left Poetry to untangle himself from his horned, yellow-stomached bullhead, while I started off after Shorty and his horned, blue-backed cow to help him chase her back up to the road and across the bridge.

But my first impression about her disposition was right. She *was* wild. She was in shallower water now, and she kept on right in it, in spite of my chasing along the shore after her and prodding her with my fishing pole and ordering her to get out of the water and head toward the road, up the ditch, and onto the bridge.

Maybe she heard the word *bridge*, though, because at last she made a splashing beeline for it—not up to the road to go across it but straight up the branch to it. Then she went *under* the bridge, where I knew the water was deeper and where many a time I'd seen hundreds of chubs and silversides and smaller minnows playing in the riffle.

"We'll get her now!" Shorty puffed behind me. "There's a fence under there on the other side. If I can catch her by the halter, we'll lead her across if we have to drag her."

But old bossy had different ideas. That old fence on the other side, which had been a nuisance to us boys many a time when we had wanted to wade around under the bridge, and which had kept all the livestock that pastured in the woods from getting through, was just like so much spider web to her.

She charged under the bridge, splashing water all over herself and everywhere, and ignored the fence as if it wasn't there—which it wasn't after she hit it head-on. In a few wire-squeaking seconds she was running like a wild thing up the steep bank and out into the woods I had come through just a little while ago myself.

Whew! And for land's sakes! If I had been on the comics page of the newspaper that comes every day to Theodore Collins's mailbox, I would have had question marks and exclamation points shooting out of my head.

Just then I heard a woman's voice coming from the direction of my house, quavering out across our orchard and through the woods. I knew it was Mom's voice calling me to come home. In fact, it was the same kind of call I'd heard a thousand times around our farm when I was quite a way from the house and it was time to eat.

I looked at my watch to see if it was suppertime, then I looked at the sun to see if my watch was right. At the same time I noticed an empty feeling in my stomach that made it seem that was what time it really was. Supper was ready, and Mom wouldn't get to have fish fillets at all—not even fried bullhead.

I looked through the arch of the bridge I was now under and at the broken fence. The post it had been fastened to at one end was floating in the water. The current of the riffle was pulling it downstream toward me and toward the creek.

And then, Shorty, instead of appreciating that I had left off what I had been in the middle of doing, which was putting a new fishing line on my pole so that I could throw it out and catch another fish—this one probably the biggest sunfish that ever lived in Sugar Creek—well, Shorty was mad at me for trying to help him.

"Look at her go!" he cried angrily from his dry standing place up on the bank. "What'd you get her all excited for? You scared her into breaking down somebody's fence, and my father will have to pay for it, and now I never *will* catch her!"

Such appreciation!

"Oh, is that so!" I said up to him. My overalls were all splashed up, and the cuffs, which I had rolled up, were soaking wet where I'd stepped into a hole in my mad race to help him get his cow out of the branch and up onto the road and across the bridge where he wanted her.

And that boy looked down at me from his dry standing place and said, "Yes, that's so! You're the same kind of impulsive boy you *used* to be!"

Then from behind me, I heard another boy's voice saying angrily, "Oh, is that so! Well, I want you to know that Bill Collins is my best friend, and whoever insults him insults me."

Shorty's broad face looked from Poetry to me and back again to Poetry.

I saw that Poetry's eyebrows were down and his jaw was set, and I could tell he was really mad.

Then Shorty shrugged his shoulders twice in a way that would stir up the temper of even

Little Jim himself or maybe Dragonfly, who was sometimes slow to get angry. He said saucily, "You two hotheads better go on back to the creek and finish your fishing." Then he spied our big catfish, which Poetry had on his stringer, and said, "Oh, a bullpout! Well, what do you know? Didn't you ever see a bull *pout* before? Ha! Ha! Ha!"

Then he whirled and started off toward the bridge.

That fired Poetry's imagination as well as his temper, and he shouted after him:

"I never saw a purple cow—I never hope
     to see one;
  But I can tell you anyhow, I'd rather see
     than be one."

And that fired *Shorty's* temper. He stood stock-still and shouted back at Poetry:

"You are a poet, and don't know it;
  If you had whiskers, you'd be a *go-at*."

Then that short-tempered boy whirled again and went on toward the branch bridge, waddling along as though he was very proud of himself as well as disgusted with two very ordinary boys who, when they went fishing, couldn't catch anything more important than an ugly, slimy bullpout.

And that was our introduction to Shorty Long's blue cow! Also, it was the beginning of a lot of upsetting trouble for the whole Sugar Creek Gang but especially for Theodore Collins's only son.

I knew that one of the very first things the gang would have to do would be to call a meeting to decide what we'd better do about having the peace and quiet of our neighborhood interrupted. Something would *have* to be done —and done quick.

3

Poetry and I decided that, since it was suppertime, we ought to go on home as soon as we could so that our parents wouldn't worry about us being drowned, and come after us.

I wasn't worried about my wet overall legs, because they had gotten wet while I was working for a good cause. Actually, it wasn't so good, but my parents were smart enough to understand.

The only thing was, Mom had made a new rule at our house. It was that if I used a towel without washing myself carefully first, I had to wash the towel, and that rule had solved a five-year-long problem for her. She had another rule, too, and that was that if I got my overalls or other clothes soiled by being careless, I got to wash them too—free!

Sometimes when I got through washing the towel or my shirt or other clothes, though, they were almost worse than they had been, and I got to wash them over, taking a little more time and soap than I had the first time.

But, as I said, this time my soiled overalls weren't what was bothering me as I carried the great big catfish on Poetry's stringer up the dusty road toward my house. The thing that was making me make a face a boy shouldn't make was one other thing Shorty had yelled back to us just before he crossed the bridge. It was:

"You may not like my cow, but you'll get to see plenty of her before the summer is over. We've rented pasture for her in the woods right across from where the red-haired Collins boy lives."

Imagine that! Why, there never had been even a horse pasturing in that woods! Old Man Paddler, who owned it, had sort of kept it just for boys to play in. Anyway, that's the way it seemed to the gang. The only animals that had ever been in it were squirrels and cottontail rabbits and chipmunks and flying squirrels and possums and coons and skunks. And now and then a fox. And once a big black bear, which Little Jim had shot. But to have a wild-eyed blue cow running loose in that woods would spoil it!

Poetry and I hadn't tried to finish untangling our lines. Because we had both been mad at Shorty and because we liked each other a lot, Poetry had made me take the catfish, saying, "It was probably your extralarge, wriggling fishworm bait he took first, anyway. He had your hook swallowed clear down into his stomach, and mine was only hooked a little bit into his upper lip."

When he told me that, I was proud of my idea to put on those six long, wriggling worms.

And, of course, Poetry was right: that big channel cat—for that's what it was, now that I had caught it—had seen that octopus-like bait coming down toward him from the surface of the water above him. And he had said, "Oh boy! What a supper!" He had made a dive for it and swallowed it in one gulp. Almost the same second, he had seen Poetry's small, scrawny-looking worm lying there in the mud or sand or on a weed and had decided to have it for dessert. Then—well, you know the rest of that story.

At supper, Mom and Dad and Charlotte Ann listened to me tell the story. I had on dry overalls—my others were hanging outdoors on the line, not being soiled enough to have to be washed but only needing drying. If it hadn't been for Shorty Long and his wild blue cow, we'd have been a happy family.

The radio in the other room was making a lot of unnecessary noise, so I had to get up and go turn it off so they could hear my story better. And there, as I looked out the front window, I saw Shorty and his round-fronted father with two ropes fastened to a blue cow's halter!

They were being dragged along by her up the road past our house toward the wooden gate to the woods, which was up the road by the two hickory trees. They'd gotten her out of Poetry's dad's woods, and it was going to be just as Shorty had said—they were going to put her into the pasture across from the Collins boy's house.

I turned up the radio volume control till the music was deafening and Mom and Dad made a parently noise in the kitchen for me to turn it down. Then I turned it all the way off and went back to finish my kind of half-mad story about Poetry and the catfish and the blue cow.

"I congratulate you," Dad said right in the middle of my story. But being interrupted made me feel the way Mom feels sometimes when she is sewing and her needle comes unthreaded. She lets out an impatient sigh that sounds a little bit like Mixy when she hisses at a dog. I'd seen and heard Mom do it quite a few times.

"Should you sigh so disgustedly?" Dad asked.

I answered, "My needle came unthreaded."

He laughed and said with a joking voice, "You mean the arch under the bridge is the needle's eye, and the cow is the thread, and—"

"Theodore!" Mom cut in on him. "Let him finish."

So I did by telling them I didn't appreciate having Shorty call me an impulsive boy, even if maybe I was a little bit. Besides, I wasn't exactly sure what the word meant. It sounded like an insult.

"You're only impulsive at times," Mom said. "You generally think things through before you act."

"And *afterward*," Dad remarked.

I looked up from my plate of raw-fried potatoes into his gray green eyes under the shaggy, reddish brown brows that hung over his eyes like a grassy ledge on a high bank of the branch. He had a mischievous twinkle in them, so I controlled my temper and went on eating.

We had already had the blessing at the table, which we always have before we eat, sometimes doing it silently, each one of us just thinking his own prayer. So I was surprised to hear Mom say, just as we were getting ready to eat a raisin rice pudding dessert with cream on it, "I think we ought to pray about our attitudes, that we'll not make it any harder for the Longs to become Christians than it would have been if they never had met us."

I already had my spoon filled with pudding and had it halfway to my mouth when Dad answered, "Let's do it right now, then, before we forget it."

We'd done it like that before at our table but not very often, and for some reason it seemed they were wanting to pray about *Bill Collins's* attitudes—that he wouldn't hate Shorty Long and do or say something my impulsive nature oughtn't do or say.

Only Dad did the out loud praying, and I guess what he said had a little to do with the rest of what happened in this mixed-up, rough-and-tumble story.

I was thinking about things a half hour later when I was out in the barn gathering eggs and helping with the other chores.

"Hi, old Bentcomb!" I said to my favorite white leghorn hen. I noticed she was still on her nest under the log in the haymow. "Haven't you laid your egg yet? Don't you know all the other hens have already started for their roosts in the chicken house?"

I went over to see if she had laid her egg, and *swish!* Peck! Peck! Peck! Her sharp bill darted out three or four times like a snapping turtle's head, pecking me hard on the hand, and she acted as fussy as an old setting hen.

"Oh, you do, do you? You want to set? You want to go clucking around the barnyard with a whole flock of fluffy little white chickens cheeping along behind you! Well, what do you know?"

Old Bentcomb got a fussy idea like that nearly every spring.

I felt under her, and she had laid her egg all right. So I said to her, "I'll tell Mom, and she'll give you a whole nestful of eggs in a cute little house all your own up by the orchard fence beside a lot of other old lady hens."

I decided to leave the one egg so she wouldn't feel like somebody that is sewing and the needle has come unthreaded. But I thought maybe I ought to stroke her on the back of her neck just to let her know she was still my favorite hen.

I did, and *swish!* Again I got pecked really hard, which made me sigh impatiently at her and say, "Don't be so impulsive!"

And that's when I remembered part of Dad's prayer. As I got the pitchfork and threw down several forkfuls of hay, I seemed to hear him saying, "We know that Peter, one of Your best disciples, was impatient at times. Yet You loved him and made a great man out of him. And we know he also loved You,"

I never would forget that part of what Dad had said. And as I stopped for a minute to look back at Bentcomb, I said, "I still like you even if you did hurt me." And it seemed I ought to be careful not to hurt the One who made me by doing or saying something I shouldn't.

Then I went down the ladder and up to the house to put some Merthiolate on my hen-pecked hand and to tell Mom to be extranice to such an impatient farmyard fowl.

Night finally came. As I finished undressing and took a look out the south window of my upstairs room, it seemed wonderful to be alive. Spring had been here quite a while, and summer was coming fast, and everybody in our family liked everybody else in it, which is the best way for a family to go to bed at night, with everybody forgiven by everybody.

The moon was making our farm and garden look as if it was painted with silver paint. The weather was just right for growing Mom's tulips in their own bed that stretched from near the iron pitcher pump about ten or fifteen feet toward the plum tree. They had looked wonderful all day, every time I had looked at them. The onions and sweet corn and beans and peas in their rows in the garden certainly looked pretty, too, I thought. But I was almost too sleepy to appreciate them, and I knew that a certain boy would have to do a lot of work on them or they'd get smothered in weeds in no time.

Away out across the top of Old Red Addie's house, Dad's clover field, beside which we were putting up a fence to protect it from the stock, was as smooth as a green lake, like the kind we had seen up North on one of our vacations. That clover would be knee-high in another month, and we'd have to cut it and put it up for hay.

Dad certainly was an interesting farmer, I thought. He was always trying some new kind of crop we'd never had before. Ladino clover was the kind he had out in the field, the kind that—and then, *wham!* Just like that, an impulsive thought socked me and kind of scared me for a second.

The thought was: *We'd better get that fence finished as soon as possible.* If we didn't, somebody's blue cow might ignore the two strands of wire we had stretched along the side of it now, and we'd wake up some morning to find half the field trampled and that same blue cow's paunch puffed up as big as a three-foot-wide balloon!

I was still sleepy though, and pretty soon I was lying on Mom's nice fresh white sheets, and pretty soon after that it was a nice sunshiny morning.

One of the first things I did, as soon as I got a chance that first day after meeting Shorty and his cow friend, was to look up in Dad's dictionary two new words I had learned yesterday. One of them was *impulsive*, and that meant "having the power of driving or impelling; easily excited to sudden action."

So, I thought, that's what Shorty Long thinks I am—easily excited to sudden action! Well, I knew somebody's wild-eyed cow that was impulsive, too!

I wasn't sure about the other half of the meaning of *impulsive*, though—the half that said "the power of driving." I'd tried to drive Shorty's cow out of the branch and up a hill and, instead, had driven her through a needle's eye and a rusty wire fence and out into the woods!

I turned in the dictionary back to the A's and found the word *attitude*, which I was supposed to be careful of. And the dictionary said "state of mind, behavior." Well, when a boy stirs you all up inside and makes you impulsive, how can you be sure you can behave yourself?

Anyway, I decided to watch myself all day, if I could.

The gang was supposed to meet at two o'clock at the Black Widow Stump above the spring—all of us who could—but I worked around the place all morning, helping Dad with the posthole digging, hoeing in the garden, and especially helping Mom get old Bentcomb out of the haymow and into her coop by the orchard fence. I had to wear gloves to do that, because she was as cross as anything.

I eased her up to the small door in the

front of the coop and let her look the situation over. It certainly was an inviting nest, with all those pretty white leghorn eggs in a round straw-lined nest just waiting for her.

I think Bentcomb must have imagined herself with fifteen little white fluffy chicks following her around, because, after she had looked for a while, she slowly started to move in, lifting each foot carefully and stepping in as if she was walking on eggs. Then she settled herself down, facing the door, and fluffed out her wings till she was twice as wide as usual. And then she looked back out at me as much as to say, "There, Bill Collins! Try to get me off this nest, and see what you get."

I didn't try it, of course, but I thought— since she was my favorite hen friend—I ought to say something nice to her. So I said, "Good-bye, madam, I'll see you again in three weeks. I congratulate you, and I wish you the best of success."

Of course, she might not get to be the mother of more than nine or ten chickens, but that would be the eggs' fault and not hers. Also, it wouldn't actually be good-bye for three whole weeks, because every day Mom let our setting hens off their nests for exercise and to eat and to get a little change. Sometimes, though, they were stubborn and didn't want to leave the coop when she wanted them to, and she had to use force.

And when they did get off, were they ever impulsive! They were no sooner out of their coops than they spread their wings and half flew and half ran, like a storm of excited feathers, out across the barnyard, squawking and cackling and flapping their wings, trying to get all their exercise at once. Then they'd rush to whatever water or food they could find and would drink and eat as if they were half starved to death.

To give old Bentcomb a last word of encouragement, I reached in to stroke her on the back of the neck again, and *wham!* Six sharp pecks landed in fast succession, hurting like everything. I drew back, quicker than scat, looking at my hand and exclaiming to her impulsively, "I certainly don't like your attitude!"

Two o'clock finally came, and I had finished the last piece of work my parents wanted me to do before it was time to meet the gang. The folks always tried to cooperate with the gang whenever they could. I would have only two hours, though, they told me.

It was like being let off a nestful of leghorn eggs, the way I shot out of our house and across the yard toward our mailbox, across the road, over the fence, and onto the path that leads to the spring. I was even imagining myself to be an old setting hen. I was flapping my arms with my powerful biceps and cackling and squawking and feeling wonderful to be alive.

Would any of the rest of the gang get there first? And would anything interesting happen during the afternoon? Also, what would we decide to do about Shorty Long and his blue cow?

4

For some reason I was the first one to get to the spring. While I was waiting, I decided to take a peek at several birds' nests I had found the week before. One of them was a bulky nest made of bark, leaves, and grass. It was hidden in one of the evergreens that bordered the rail fence between the woods and the bayou.

I crept up cautiously, hoping to find Mama Cardinal on her nest of several pale gray eggs with chocolate markings. Sure enough, she was. She was not as beautiful as her bright red, black-throated husband, but she was pretty. She was more of a grayish brown, although her kind of proud-looking head was red like her wings and tail.

I stood stock-still when I saw her, not moving a muscle, not even flexing my biceps as I had been doing more or less all morning and afternoon. I stood there, poised like a pointer dog that has just discovered a covey of quail.

One of the prettiest sounds a boy ever hears around Sugar Creek is a cardinal in a tree somewhere whistling a cheery "Cheo-cheo-chehoo-cheo." I was hoping I would hear one any minute, which would mean that the mother cardinal's husband was somewhere around. But he was probably busy or else was high in a tree watching *me* to see if I would be dumb enough to scare his wife off her nest.

"I commend you," I said to her as I caught her eye just above a little tuft of what looked like bluegrass. "I wish you the best of success."

Then I stepped carefully back and went on to see how a mother robin was getting along. Her mud-lined nest of dry grass and twigs was in the crotch of an elm tree near a big patch of mayapples with large, spreading, shining, light green leaves. But Mother Robin not only didn't stay on her nest when I crept up to take a look, but she and her husband and about a dozen neighbor robins started to give me one of the worst scoldings I'd ever had. It seemed they were all around me and above me, ordering me to get out and stay out. *"Quick! Quick!"* All of them were screaming the same thing.

"OK, *OK!*" I said disgustedly. "Give me a *chance!*" And I got myself out of there as quick as I could. *Such* a neighborhood!

I found out right away why Poetry was late to our meeting when I saw him swinging along, on one shoulder happily carrying something about four feet long, and grinning broadly.

"What you got there?" I asked.

"Birthday present for the biggest fish that has *never* been caught."

As soon as I got to where he was, I saw it was a new minnow net of carefully woven twine, probably cotton, having what looked like six or eight meshes to every inch of length. When he unrolled it, it was about three yards long. It had dozens of properly spaced lead sinkers at the bottom and plenty of wooden floats at the top.

"What do you mean, 'the *biggest* fish'?" I asked him. "If you ask me, I'd say minnows are the *smallest* fish."

"Minnows for *bait*," he said. "We're going after bass next time—not somebody's little old yellow-stomached catfish!"

He was in a cheerful mood, and so was I, in spite of having been driven out of a whole neighborhood of noisy robins. "Where you going to get the minnows?" I asked him.

He answered, "Under the bridge in the branch."

Well, I'd been under that bridge before, and for a different reason, so I said, "If there are any minnows left, after being half scared to death by Shorty's nonsensical cow!"

Pretty soon, Big Jim came. I looked secretly at his mustache and, still more secretly, at mine, using a small pocket mirror. I could see that I really didn't even have any fuzz—not even as much as a baby pigeon has on its awkward body when it is just hatched and has had a chance to dry a little.

I looked at Big Jim's biceps too, which he was always feeling to see if they were as hard as he wanted them to be. And when I looked back at the one on my right arm, it was actually bulging a little, like a pullet egg, and it seemed to be getting harder! Spying a branch extending out from a tree trunk beside me, I leaped up and started chinning myself, managing to do it ten times before I got tired.

"It's your feet that make you so heavy," Poetry squawked, and he quoted a little poem he was always quoting when he got a chance or when anything made him think of it:

"A centipede was happy, quite,
   Until a frog, in fun,
   Said, 'Pray, which leg comes after which?'
   This roused her mind to such a pitch,
   She lay distracted in the ditch,
   Considering how to run."

"The centipede lay in the ditch, or the frog?" I asked Poetry. Whirling around, I used a wrestling trick I knew, and in a tangled-up second he was sprawled on the ground. If there had been a ditch there, he would have been lying in it, considering how to run.

Pretty soon after that, Little Jim came moseying along, swinging his ash stick and grinning and socking the tops of weeds and mayapples and looking as if he didn't have a trouble in the world.

"Hi, everybody!" he said to us, and we said, "Hi!" back to him.

In only a few more minutes, Circus loped up the path that runs from the big Sugar Creek bridge to the spring, and we were all there except Dragonfly and Little Tom Till, who generally is not able to meet with the gang as often as the rest of us.

I looked at Poetry, and he had a stubborn look on his face. "Have you ever thought where she'll have to get her drinking water?" he asked savagely with his squawky voice. "Do we want somebody's cow walking around in the mud all around the spring? Do we want her to thrust her cow's nose into the same cement pool we put our lips into when we lie down and drink? Do we want her to make a barnyard out of our nice cool resting place? I, for one, don't like the idea!" He finished with a very stormy voice.

What he had said certainly made the situation seem a lot worse than it had.

But Little Jim, who always liked to take anybody's part, chimed in. "Paul Bunyan had a blue cow named Babe, and everybody liked both of them."

Poetry came back with a saucy answer, saying gruffly, "Paul Bunyan was a *mythical* character. But this cow's not imaginary. She's got real horns and doesn't have any sense. She tore through the fence my father had under the bridge and that had kept our horses and cows from going through for years and years. In one-fifth of a second she tore it down and went storming out into our woods! I hate to think what she'll do to our playground if she stays here all summer. And that dumb *boy! Honestly!*"

Poetry was sitting beside his unrolled minnow net. His jaw was set, and his eyebrows were down in a scowl as he finished.

Big Jim was getting warmed up, too, I could see. Poetry had introduced a few ideas we

Big Jim looked at his watch and said, "Anybody seen Roy?"

"Roy *who?*" Little Jim asked with a mischievous grin in his voice and on his face. It did sound strange, hearing anybody call Dragonfly by his birthday name, which nobody but his mother and father used when they talked to him.

Well, we waited around quite a while, rolling in the grass and listening to Poetry's and my stories about the monster catfish and the six night crawlers on one hook and the blue cow that had come charging in on our fishing privacy. And about Shorty Long, who had moved back to our neighborhood.

That was one thing we always had to decide whenever a new boy moved in—whether or not he could belong to our gang and what to do if he was bullheaded, or a bully, or a sissy, or was stuck-up, or wasn't quite a human being. Sometimes, without any of us wanting to, someone from the gang got into a fight with the new boy, which helped us get acquainted right away—or a little quicker, anyhow.

I had already had my fight with Shorty over a year ago. We had made up at least partway but still were not able to like each other very well for some reason.

After we had waited another ten minutes for Dragonfly, who knew we were having the meeting and should have been there, we decided to go ahead and have it without him.

"Maybe it would be better anyway," Circus

said, "the way Shorty got Dragonfly against the rest of us when he lived here before."

Poetry, who was lying on his side in front of me, rose up on his elbow and asked, "Are we going to stand for having our gang almost broken up?"

Big Jim's narrowed eyes said no without the lips under his almost mustache saying a word.

"And what about his blue cow?" Poetry asked again.

Big Jim answered that for us. "I'm afraid that's out of our hands. Old Man Paddler has rented this woods to the Long family, and it's a simple business arrangement between them."

"But what if she comes charging wildly into whatever we're doing!" Poetry exclaimed. "We don't have to stand for *that!*"

I didn't realize that the members of our gang knew so much about what to do with a wild cow until different ones said what they thought was the best thing to do.

Little Jim spoke up first. "You can have the rubber grips off my bicycle handlebars. If you slip them over her horns, they won't be so sharp and hurt so much if she runs into you headfirst."

I looked at his small serious face, and he had really meant it.

Big Jim answered, "They do make such things—'Safety Rubber Horn Protectors,' I believe they call them. I saw them advertised in a farm magazine. That's a good idea. It might protect Shorty himself. I understand she has to

be milked twice a day, and if she's as w say she is, she might gore him to death

That seemed to be a nice attitude, I And there ran through my mind an id not only ought to grow a mustache the Jim was doing faster than any of the rest and develop my biceps till they were as b as hard and maybe even stronger than his I ought to *really* watch my attitude toward S Long. It ought to be as kind as Big Jim sh his was right that minute.

Circus spoke up then, taking somet out of his hip pocket at the same time. "I fo this in our barn. It was kind of rusty, but I sa papered it and oiled it and wiped it off a cleaned it up, and it works. If we can get it into her nose, she'll be as meek as a lamb."

I looked at what he had, and it was what farmers call a "cattle lead," the kind that snaps into a cow's nose but not the kind that pierces the cow's nostrils. As Circus worked the co spring up and down and opened the jaws an closed them again, I started to grin to myself I imagined how, if we could get the lead snapp into Shorty's blue cow's nose, anybody co lead her across a noisy-floored bridge or where. Then we wouldn't have to drive her a club or a whip or a long cane fishing p throw rocks at her or scream at her and her wilder than ever.

Of course, if she had an honest-to-go *bull* ring in her nose that couldn't eve out, she'd really be safe.

Big Jim looked at his watch and said, "Any-body seen Roy?"

"Roy *who?*" Little Jim asked with a mis-chievous grin in his voice and on his face. It did sound strange, hearing anybody call Dragonfly by his birthday name, which nobody but his mother and father used when they talked to him.

Well, we waited around quite a while, rolling in the grass and listening to Poetry's and my stories about the monster catfish and the six night crawlers on one hook and the blue cow that had come charging in on our fishing privacy. And about Shorty Long, who had moved back to our neighborhood.

That was one thing we always had to decide whenever a new boy moved in—whether or not he could belong to our gang and what to do if he was bullheaded, or a bully, or a sissy, or was stuck-up, or wasn't quite a human being. Some-times, without any of us wanting to, someone from the gang got into a fight with the new boy, which helped us get acquainted right away—or a little quicker, anyhow.

I had already had my fight with Shorty over a year ago. We had made up at least partway but still were not able to like each other very well for some reason.

After we had waited another ten minutes for Dragonfly, who knew we were having the meeting and should have been there, we decid-ed to go ahead and have it without him.

"Maybe it would be better anyway," Circus

said, "the way Shorty got Dragonfly against the rest of us when he lived here before."

Poetry, who was lying on his side in front of me, rose up on his elbow and asked, "Are we going to stand for having our gang almost broken up?"

Big Jim's narrowed eyes said no without the lips under his almost mustache saying a word.

"And what about his blue cow?" Poetry asked again.

Big Jim answered that for us. "I'm afraid that's out of our hands. Old Man Paddler has rented this woods to the Long family, and it's a simple business arrangement between them."

"But what if she comes charging wildly into whatever we're doing!" Poetry exclaimed. "We don't have to stand for *that!*"

I didn't realize that the members of our gang knew so much about what to do with a wild cow until different ones said what they thought was the best thing to do.

Little Jim spoke up first. "You can have the rubber grips off my bicycle handlebars. If you slip them over her horns, they won't be so sharp and hurt so much if she runs into you headfirst."

I looked at his small serious face, and he had really meant it.

Big Jim answered, "They do make such things—'Safety Rubber Horn Protectors,' I believe they call them. I saw them advertised in a farm magazine. That's a good idea. It might protect Shorty himself. I understand she has to be milked twice a day, and if she's as wild as you say she is, she might gore him to death."

That seemed to be a nice attitude, I thought. And there ran through my mind an idea that I not only ought to grow a mustache the way Big Jim was doing faster than any of the rest of us—and develop my biceps till they were as big and as hard and maybe even stronger than his—but I ought to *really* watch my attitude toward Shorty Long. It ought to be as kind as Big Jim showed his was right that minute.

Circus spoke up then, taking something out of his hip pocket at the same time. "I found this in our barn. It was kind of rusty, but I sand-papered it and oiled it and wiped it off and cleaned it up, and it works. If we can get it in her nose, she'll be as meek as a lamb."

I looked at what he had, and it was wl farmers call a "cattle lead," the kind that snaps into a cow's nose but not the kind that pierces the cow's nostrils. As Circus worked the coil spring up and down and opened the jaws and closed them again, I started to grin to myself as I imagined how, if we could get the lead snapped into Shorty's blue cow's nose, anybody could lead her across a noisy-floored bridge or any-where. Then we wouldn't have to drive her with a club or a whip or a long cane fishing pole or throw rocks at her or scream at her and make her wilder than ever.

Of course, if she had an honest-to-goodness *bull* ring in her nose that couldn't ever come out, she'd really be safe.

I looked at Poetry, and he had a stubborn look on his face. "Have you ever thought where she'll have to get her drinking water?" he asked savagely with his squawky voice. "Do we want somebody's cow walking around in the mud all around the spring? Do we want her to thrust her cow's nose into the same cement pool we put our lips into when we lie down and drink? Do we want her to make a barnyard out of our nice cool resting place? I, for one, don't like the idea!" He finished with a very stormy voice.

What he had said certainly made the situation seem a lot worse than it had.

But Little Jim, who always liked to take anybody's part, chimed in. "Paul Bunyan had a blue cow named Babe, and everybody liked both of them."

Poetry came back with a saucy answer, saying gruffly, "Paul Bunyan was a *mythical* character. But this cow's not imaginary. She's got real horns and doesn't have any sense. She tore through the fence my father had under the bridge and that had kept our horses and cows from going through for years and years. In one-fifth of a second she tore it down and went storming out into our woods! I hate to think what she'll do to our playground if she stays here all summer. And that dumb *boy! Honestly!*"

Poetry was sitting beside his unrolled minnow net. His jaw was set, and his eyebrows were down in a scowl as he finished.

Big Jim was getting warmed up, too, I could see. Poetry had introduced a few ideas we hadn't thought of yet. Who *did* want an uncontrollable cow making a barnyard out of the nice, cool, shady place down below the linden tree where we got our drinking water and which was the only place where a cow in that woods *could* get her water?

Big Jim spoke then. "One thing we ought to decide right now—and that is, absolutely no fighting!"

I remembered what Mom had said at the lunch table, and I joined in with Big Jim's idea. "We ought to watch our attitudes. We don't want to make it any harder for the Longs to become Christians than it would have been if they had never met us."

For some reason, saying that made me feel as fine inside as I do when I see a flying squirrel sailing out from a high branch of a butternut tree and landing lightly on another branch a lot lower down. I'd seen one of those round-headed, shorthaired, short-bodied, beautiful, and very graceful little animal friends make his flying leap many a time when he got scared and wanted to get somewhere from somewhere.

All the flying squirrels around Sugar Creek are what is called "nocturnal," which means they forage around for food at night like owls, and their big eyes can also see better at night. But once in a while, one will get waked up out of its leafy nest by a boy throwing a stone and hitting it. And then it gets excited and makes a running jump with its front and back legs spread out wide. The skin that is attached to its wrists and ankles on each side makes a kind of sail, and it just flies through the air with the greatest of ease.

I get a happy feeling when I see a flying squirrel do that. I also feel fine when it lands on the ground, if it can run fast enough to get away from a dog that might be there to chase it. The very second it lands, it quickly scampers for the base of another tree and scoots up it like lightning, sometimes to the very top. If it's still scared and wants to get *farther* away, it makes another running leap and sails out again toward the foot of another tree. And when it lands again—*scoot!* Up that next tree it goes like a rusty brown streak of live lightning. Or, if I happen to see its side instead of its back, it looks like a light brown streak.

Anyway, when I said to the gang, quoting my mother, that we ought to watch our attitudes toward Shorty Long and his parents, it made me feel as fine as if I had jumped out of a high tree, had landed safely, and was up another tree and safe myself.

From where I was lying, I could still hear the robins scolding up along the bayou fence near the patch of mayapples. In fact, all of a sudden they began to scold louder and louder, as though they had gotten their heads together, were talking it all over again, and couldn't agree on what to do about a red-haired boy who all of a sudden had come out of nowhere into the peace and quiet of their neighborhood and interrupted it. They sounded even worse and more impatient than they had when I had been there.

And then, all of another sudden, I knew they weren't scolding about Bill Collins at all, for from that same direction there came the sound of running feet, loud enough and fast enough to have been made by a centipede as big as a circus elephant, one that knew exactly how to run. It also sounded like a windstorm.

Rolling over quick and looking up along the bayou fence, I saw a chubby boy and a skinny one, hanging onto a rope apiece. The other ends of the ropes were attached to the halter of a scrawny-looking, half-scared-to-death blue cow that was dragging them along on an impatient run straight toward us, breaking into the privacy of an innocent gang meeting the way she had done yesterday to a peaceful fishing adventure.

One of the boys being dragged along against his will—which I knew was sometimes very stubborn—was Dragonfly Gilbert, the pop-eyed member of the Sugar Creek Gang, whose nose turns south at the end and who is allergic to almost everything and who is also a great little guy.

The boy on the end of the other rope was as barrel-shaped as Poetry, but his mind wasn't any more like Poetry's than the man in the moon.

In another second, the blue cow, which didn't seem to realize what she was doing or where she was going—only that she was trying to keep from being stopped from doing something—that blue cow would cut a path right through our little huddle, and we'd get pretty badly hurt.

So most of us yelled, "Watch out! Everybody *scatter!*"

We did, and just in time, as a blue tornado followed by two different-sized boys went tearing madly past!

And that's where Poetry's nice, new, six-mesh-to-the-inch, nine-foot-long minnow net with lead weights on one end and large wooden floats on the other helped make matters even worse.

Swish, double-swish, swooshety! What on earth was happening?

Not only the four feet of that cow—each foot having two hooves, making a total of eight—but somehow the horns on her head also got tangled up in that strong-meshed net. And then she got mixed up in her mind, not knowing how to run, and down she went with Dragonfly and Shorty doing almost the same thing.

And *that* was the rest of the gang's getting its introduction to the strange wild animal along with the boy who was supposed to take care of her.

I don't know how long the centipede in the poem lay distracted in the ditch, considering how to run, before it came to its senses, put its many legs to work again, and ran on. But it certainly didn't take that scared cow long to get going again. In seconds, she was putting her four legs to work, getting up hind feet first, the way cows always do, and accidentally trampling Poetry's nice new minnow net into the ground.

Then, like a shot she was off in the direction of the linden tree, with Dragonfly and Shorty still holding onto their ropes and whirling along after her. The three of them resembled a terribly big blue kite with two kite tails dangling and tossing around in a windstorm.

And was Poetry ever mad!

We all were mad only a few seconds later when she reached the linden tree above the spring, and both Shorty and Dragonfly stumbled and fell and let go.

Down the steep incline she shot, all the way to the spring itself, with all of us up and after her. And I was imagining what would happen to our nice clear pool of sparkling drinking water, having seen her land yesterday with her four feet in the branch and charge up it, under the bridge and through the fence on the other side!

What would I see when I got to the spring?

A minute later most of us were at the top of the incline, expecting to see most anything, such as a blue cow lying on her side with a broken leg. Or maybe she would have charged right on through the drinking pool, through the mud on the other side, and through the two-strand barbed-wire fence. By this time she might be halfway up the path that led to the other side of the bayou.

It was an astonishing sight that we saw. There, standing with her front feet right in the middle of the cement pool and with her hind feet in six inches of mud, was our four-footed, blue-haired mammal. Her sides were heaving from running so hard, and she had her nose thrust into the water and was trying to drink and swallow between breaths.

"Wonderful!" Shorty cried with a happy voice from behind me. "That's what we'd been trying to get her to do! She wouldn't go down the hill to drink, and she would have starved to death for water. We were trying to lead her!"

"But look at what she's done!" Poetry cried. "Look at our paper drinking cups—all smashed and squashed to nothing! Look at our wooden bench upside down in the mud! Look at her muddy feet standing in the middle of our drinking water!"

And before anybody could have stopped him, Poetry was working his way down that steep slope on the left side and yelling, "Get out of there with those muddy feet, you— you—"

It was hard to believe that Poetry was so mad, because he was nearly always so happy-go-lucky. But when I remembered *he* had made the little wooden bench that had been beside the pool and had also painted it himself—Poetry was especially good at carpentry and was always making something out of wood with his set of carpenter's tools—well, his temper was easy to understand.

But then Mrs. Cow, seeing us and seeing and hearing Poetry charging down the hill at her, came to life. She pivoted and started up the incline on the other side of the linden tree. I knew that in another moment she would be up the slope, and, if nobody stopped her, she would be racing through the woods again. Like Little Bo Peep's sheep, she would have her tail behind her, but also she would have the two ropes dangling from her halter.

Then things *really* began to happen. Those two ropes got mixed up with her feet and hooves. She stepped on one of them with one of her front feet, the other with one of her hind feet, and got stopped in her tracks. The ropes were caught between her cloven hooves. She lunged forward and was down again.

That's when Circus, our acrobat, went into action. Like an arrow, he was down the incline on the other side, and as quick as a cowboy racing to a cow he has lassoed, he was down there with his cow lead open. Catching her with his left hand by one of her horns, he was struggling to snap the lead into her nostrils.

"Help me, one of you guys!" he cried back up to us. "I can't hold her!"

Big Jim ran to help. He was down that incline like another arrow, and in a flash they had that cow lead snapped into her nostrils. They got one of the ropes off her halter and snapped into the ring in the lead's handle.

And Shorty's wild cow was in captivity.

5

It took me almost a week to get over the excitement of that one afternoon. Shorty's cow never did get over it. If she had been afraid to go down that hill to get her drinking water before, she was more than ever scared after that experience.

Our problem was solved as far as her making a barnyard out of our nice cool resting place was concerned, but how to get water for her was another problem. We couldn't let her die of thirst.

And that's why, because I lived right across the road from her pasture, I borrowed one of Mom's oldest washtubs and set it just inside her fence straight across the road from our mailbox in the shade of an elderberry bush. Every morning and night I carried a pail of water or two from our iron pitcher pump and poured it into the tub for her to drink. Shorty let me do it without even bothering to say thank you.

Of course, we couldn't leave Circus's cow lead in her nose or she would be too nervous and wouldn't give much milk—which she didn't anyway for almost a week after such an exciting experience.

Poetry got his minnow net untangled all right. It wasn't hurt much—just torn in a few places. And as the spring days raced along, we had lots of fun with it, seining and wading in the branch and actually catching several large bass, using minnows for bait.

If Shorty's blue cow had only showed a little appreciation for all I was doing for her, I'd have felt better about it. But her attitude was anything but polite. I kept on carrying water for her and alfalfa for her to eat, and she had so much bluegrass all day long that you'd have thought she would have been a contented cow. But she wasn't.

She was still wild. Whenever any of us got anywhere near her in the woods, she would lift her horned head, spread her blue, hair-fringed ears wide, and stare. Then, like a deer, she would wheel and dash, with her tail switching over her back, into the bushes. And it didn't make any difference what bushes. Wild rose-bushes with pretty flowers on them got trampled, chokecherry shrubs got knocked down and smashed into the ground, and even the ground under our papaw bushes, which she used as a hiding place to get away from the flies, began to look like a barnyard.

Our playground was really being spoiled.

But Shorty himself was our worst trouble. Again, he made a special friend out of Dragonfly, and it was kind of like a big hen with one little spindle-legged chicken following her wherever she went.

I overheard them talking one day when they were alone, and what they were saying made me feel sad and mad at the same time. My temper had been under pretty good control up until then, and I was living up to Big Jim's rule—*no fighting*. But it certainly didn't feel good to realize that our gang was being divided, not only by Shorty's making a close pal out of Dragonfly but by his almost making a bad boy out of him.

I happened to be alone down at the mouth of the branch at the time, waiting for Poetry to come and fish with me as he had before. I'd had six or seven or maybe eight fishing worms wrapping themselves around the shank of my hook for maybe thirty minutes and hadn't had even a nibble.

Poetry would be there pretty soon, I thought, and then we would seine a few minnows, and maybe we could tempt a bass or a goggle-eye or something.

That's when, all of a sudden, I heard somebody giggle in the bushes behind me. I knew it was Dragonfly's voice—especially since right that second I heard him sneeze. And then I heard Shorty start talking about stuff a boy as young as Dragonfly shouldn't even know about. It was like somebody pouring melted garbage into my ears, and I really fired up. (That was another rule of the gang. We never used any filthy language or laughed at anybody's dirty jokes if we happened to overhear any.)

What Shorty had said was something about one of Circus's many sisters, the one named Lucille. She was the one who would smile back at me across the schoolroom. She wouldn't make fun of me if for some reason—when she was around—I strengthened my biceps by chinning myself with my sleeves rolled up to my shoulders or turned a handspring and accidentally bumped my nose on the ground.

Well, when I heard Shorty's voice saying what he was saying, and I knew who he was saying it about, and hearing Dragonfly giggle as if he himself thought it was funny, well, my long cane fishing pole with its strong line and its wriggling night crawlers on its hook went *kersplash* into the water. I didn't even take time to set the pole.

I scrambled to my feet, every nerve in my body alive with temper, and every drop of blood in my veins tingling. I started on a firm-footed march toward the big elm tree behind which I guessed the boys were.

In seconds I was where they were lying on the mashed-down bluegrass. With my two fists so tight the knuckles were white, I looked down at Shorty and demanded, "You—you low-minded, foulmouthed skunk! Say that again!" My voice was trembling, I noticed, but it wasn't from fear.

"It's the truth!" he said, and he was over on his side and up on his knees and his feet in a flash.

And the rule about no fighting was broken into a thousand pieces.

My right arm shot out, and, with the hardest-knuckled fist I ever had, I socked him right in the center of his jaw. I saw his head jerk back, his eyes go glassy, and his knees buckle, and he went down like a cornstalk that has been run over by a spring-toothed harrow.

He landed in a tangled-up scramble of arms and legs and groaned and lay still.

Dragonfly looked at him with his pop-eyes and cried, "You—you've killed him! You've killed him!"

I was down on my knees beside Shorty in a second, trembling with temper and fear, feeling proud that I could hit so hard but also feeling sorry. It took me only a second more to see that he was still breathing.

I quickly grabbed up Dragonfly's straw hat, which was lying there, raced to the branch, and came back with it full of water—half full, that is, because of most of it had leaked through the straw as though the hat was a sieve. I started sprinkling it on Shorty's face, and in almost no time he came to, groaning and complaining and holding his jaw and his head.

"I've got a headache!" he said. "Oh—" And he groaned and rolled over and doubled up as if he also had cramps from having eaten too many green grapes or apples or something.

Just then I heard running steps, and Poetry's voice called from the creek behind me, "Where *are* you? You've got a fish on your line! Come and get him!"

Realizing Shorty wasn't injured—not seriously, anyway—I yelled to Poetry, "I'm back here. I just landed a big one. Come and help me!"

"You come and catch the one on your line!" Poetry called. "I can't hold him."

"A fish in the bushes is worth two in the creek!" I cried back to him. But then, looking down at Shorty's disgusting-looking face and the mouth out of which so many slimy words had come, I pitied him—not because I had licked him with one powerful sock but because of the kind of mind he had.

Behind me at the creek I could hear Poetry struggling, and I knew I'd rather be with him catching the fish he said was on my line. But I couldn't go just yet. I had something more important to do.

"Get up!" I ordered Shorty, standing there with my doubled-up fists and my bent elbows ready to plunge into another fight if I had to. "I said, get up!" I ordered him again.

He rolled over two or three times in the direction of the branch, and then, with his eyes on me the way a rooster in a fight looks at another rooster that has been licking him, he got to his feet.

With my feet carefully easing me and my flexed biceps and my set jaw toward him, I was waiting for one move that would show me he was going to fight back.

But he started to walk backward, still eyeing me, and I decided to stay where I was and see what happened.

When he was maybe fifteen feet from me in the direction of the branch bridge, he got a stubborn expression on his face and a sarcastic tone in his voice and called to Dragonfly, "Come on, Roy! Let's get out of here! Let's leave these goody-goody boys to themselves!"

When Dragonfly, who was now standing and looking worried, didn't come, he yelled at him, "I said, come on!"

And the thundery voice brought Dragonfly to life. He swept up his straw hat from the ground and started toward the bridge after his friend.

"Stay where you are!"

My own thundery voice socked Dragonfly's ears, and he stopped, looking like a baby rabbit being held in a boy's hand, trembling and not knowing what to do.

"You've got to *choose!*" Shorty's voice sounded braver than it had, maybe because he was now even farther away.

The expression on Dragonfly's face was almost pitiful, and I knew that for some reason he was afraid of what might happen to him if he didn't do what Shorty Long ordered!

He looked up at me, and for a second I thought I saw in his eyes the very special expression he'd had many a time when he liked me. But then, as if he had decided something, he came to life. As Shorty started off on a run, Dragonfly broke into a run of his own right after him.

From behind me, Poetry was yelling, "I've got him! He's another channel cat! What's the matter with you? Come *on!*"

But I couldn't go. I just stood as if I was

glued to the spot where, a few minutes before, Shorty's socked jaw had been lying. My eyes were focused on two boys—a spindle-legged one and a short, chubby one. Running.

Up the hill at the side of the bridge they went and onto the noisy wooden bridge itself, where they stopped and looked back for only a second. Then they went on, and I noticed that Shorty had his arm across Dragonfly's shoulder as if they were pals, and they were talking as they went.

When I got back to where Poetry was just putting what looked like a three-pound channel cat onto his stringer, I could hardly see for some reason.

He looked up at me and said, "What's the matter? What you got tears in your eyes for?"

We didn't catch a single other fish. In fact, we didn't even seine any minnows, because after I told him what had happened back in the bushes while he was landing the catfish, neither one of us felt much like being happy. So after we tried for thirty minutes or more to land another fish of just any kind, we gave up and started for home.

Besides, it would soon be time to start doing the chores, such things as gathering the eggs and watering the stock, including Shorty's cow.

I made Poetry take the big fish this time. "You caught it," I insisted when he objected.

He finally gave in, and I was glad he did, because the proud expression on his face as he carried the big fish, which looked bigger and bigger as we walked along, was something to see.

When we got to the middle of the branch bridge, Poetry and I stopped for a few jiffies, lay down on our different-sized stomachs, and looked over the edge at the new fence he and his father had put there and at the scores of chubs and shiners and different kinds of minnows that were swimming in the lively water.

Then we stood up, and all of a sudden Poetry said, "Let's be friends forever."

When I didn't say anything except "Uh-huh," which meant I'd rather be that than anything else in the world, he put his arm across my shoulders, and we walked the rest of the way across the bridge and up the hill toward the lane that branches off toward their toolshed and their barn and house.

When I got home, Dad wasn't there, having gone somewhere in the car and not being back yet. So without anybody to tell me to, I dived into the chores, getting them done faster than usual.

I was all the way up the haymow ladder and looking in the corner under the log for old Bentcomb's egg before I remembered that she was cooped up out by the orchard fence. Her three weeks must be almost over, I thought as I tossed a few balls at the basketball hoop Dad and I had fixed there.

Mixy had her eye on my egg bucket as I came down the ladder, not knowing for sure what was in it and walking along in little jerky runs, back and forth and all around me. She was meowing and meowing hungrily, as she does when we have just milked old Jersey Jill and she knows she'll probably get a little in her tin pan by the cabinet.

"Nothing but eggs," I said to her, holding the pail down for her to stick her black-and-white nose into and see—and maybe smell—for herself.

She took one short peek, then walked with upright tail to her pan by Dad's cabinet. While going past, I happened to see another new book that he had bought. He had joined the "Farm Book of the Month Club," I had found out, which was why his shelf of books was growing so fast.

Spying the one called *A Veterinary Handbook for the Average Farmer, or What to Do Before the Doctor Arrives,* I was reminded that it had a chapter in it about diet for milk cows. I took a quick look through that chapter, and that's when I got the idea to try to make up for Shorty's sore jaw.

All the time since I'd started the chores, I'd been remembering what Mom had said about watching our attitudes. I had really tried and had been a fairly good boy in spite of myself. But less than an hour ago, my attitude had been like a Sugar Creek tornado. Part of me had gone tearing into Shorty, knocking the living daylights out of him, and part of me had stood still and felt proud of me while I did it.

It seemed what I had done was right—but it also seemed it was wrong. I really couldn't tell for sure. But I decided if there *was* anything wrong about it that I couldn't see yet, I'd ask God to forgive me for it and to please fix my heart up so that it would feel good again inside.

I was carrying a pail of sparkling clear water from our pitcher pump and looking at the bluegrass that seemed to be the only kind of cow diet the woods had, except for flowers and rosebushes and stuff. Then I got to thinking how Jersey Jill got to eat ensilage and chopped corn and bran, all kinds of good milk-producing food, including some of the nice new ladino clover in the field up by the pignut trees.

Thinking that, I quickly poured the water into the tub under the elderberry bush, ran back to the barn, got the sickle, and went through the nice new gate Dad and I had hung after we'd put up the big corner post my biceps had helped dig the hole for. In a few minutes I had a pitchfork heaped high with fresh-smelling green clover and was on my way with it through the front gate. A second later I was calling with my cow-calling voice and tossing that nice forkful of ladino clover over the fence for a nervous, unappreciative cow to eat for her supper.

She couldn't have been far away—I had poured in the water just a few minutes before, and now, when I looked into the tub, I noticed she had drunk almost half a tubful while I had been up cutting the clover. Maybe I had forgotten to water her that morning. I wasn't sure.

She came kind of hesitantly toward the fence, again eyeing me suspiciously, as much as to say, "I don't trust you." When she got to within a few feet of the fresh clover, she sniffed as if she was going to turn up her nose at it and maybe refuse to even touch it. But just one taste of that clover and she went after it as though she was half starved.

As I stood there with my pitchfork over my shoulder, watching her, it seemed I was feeling a little better inside. And for a second I half *liked* her and felt sorry for her for being such a lonesome cow without a friend in the world.

Dad came driving up about that time, and, seeing what I had done, he warned me, "It won't hurt her if she already has a lot of bluegrass in her stomach, but be careful you don't feed her or any other cow a lot of that ladino clover when it's wet with dew or feed her on an empty stomach. She'd blow up like a dirigible. Harm Groenwald lost two heifers on just plain white clover this morning. They died in thirty minutes after they started to bloat."

"I didn't give her very much," I said. "Just a small forkful. That won't hurt her, will it?"

Dad drove on into the drive and then came back and stood with me, watching. "Better take a little of it away. I wouldn't want anything bad to happen. The dew sometimes falls early this time of year. That clover looks pretty wet."

I didn't want anything to happen either, so

71

I climbed over the fence with my pitchfork and started to take away some of the hay. But that cow was stubborn. She wouldn't budge, and I had to turn the fork around and tap her with it to make her get out of the way so that I could toss the hay back on our side of the fence.

"Get back out of the way!" I ordered her.

But she wouldn't take orders. She liked that hay and was going to have it or else. It might not be dangerously wet with dew, but she had just drunk a lot of water, and it would certainly get wet inside of her. And when her stomach started churning it around, it would cause gas aplenty.

Shorty *would* have to come running through the woods at just that same time, yelling, "Hey, you! Let my cow alone! Don't you *dare* stick her with that pitchfork!"

"I'm trying to save her life," I exclaimed to him.

He thundered back, "You don't save cows' lives by jabbing them with pitchforks!" He rushed against me, whamming me in the side with his hip and bowling me over.

I landed in the shade of the elderberry bush and in what was left of the water his blue cow hadn't finished drinking.

I could feel my attitude blowing up like a dirigible, and I was getting the temper bloat worse than any cow could have gotten cow bloat by eating white clover or alfalfa or even ladino. And before I knew it I was making short work of Shorty again.

We squared off and rushed at each other. We struck and boxed and dodged and rushed in at each other—I with my all-wet overalls seat and he with fists much bigger and harder than mine. I could tell I was licking him, though, and I kept trying for the same place on his jaw where I had hit him before and laid him out. I also was talking and half yelling to him, "You say anything rotten about Lucille Browne again, and it'll be the last time you ever talk at all!"

Even though I was licking him, Shorty didn't seem to know it, and he wouldn't quit. And the fight went on. Then for some reason I felt as if maybe I was getting licked myself. I could tell from the blood on my sleeve when I wiped my nose with it and the way I felt in about seventy-seven different places where I'd been hit.

All the time, I knew Dad was standing on the other side of the fence, watching and not saying a word. He was probably thinking plenty.

I was ashamed to get licked and was also wondering why he didn't try to stop us. It would be a good time right now if he was going to. I'd certainly be ashamed to get licked with him watching. It would have been better if he had seen the one-sock fight at the mouth of the branch an hour ago, when my biceps and my other muscles had been a lot stronger than they seemed right now.

Then I quit thinking, because our fight, which had started with a flurry of socks and whams and squishes and double whams, ended the way the other one had—with just one sock on a jaw. Only it wasn't Shorty's jaw this time, but mine! I felt things whirling round in my head like a Sugar Creek whirlwind, and then I felt myself being sucked down into a dizzying black world. I was knocked out and didn't know it.

When I came to, Dad was sprinkling water on my face from Mom's washtub under the elderberry bush, the same water that quite a while ago a blue cow had had her nervous nose in.

I sat up and looked groggily around. I didn't see Shorty or his blue cow. Mom was there, though, in the ditch on the other side of the fence. Beside her, tugging at her skirts and looking worried, was Charlotte Ann, my little sister.

Dad was grinning as he said, "I'm proud of you, son. You fought like a man. You licked him!"

I jerked my head up and looked all around to see if maybe Shorty was there somewhere on the ground and I had missed seeing him the first time I'd looked. But he wasn't.

"You fought a clean fight, and you didn't swear! You just happened to get hit too hard in the right place."

There were tears in my eyes, but with both my parents watching me, I kept them out of my voice. "Where'd he go? And where's the dumb old cow?"

"Shorty and his father have her up at the corral at the hickory trees, milking her."

"His father!" I exclaimed as I got to my feet

to see if I could still stand on them, and I could. "Did he see me get licked?"

"Not on your life. When you went down, I ordered the champion to get his cow and get out of here. He drove her up toward the corral, and his father just got there a minute ago with the pail."

I hated to look into Mom's eyes to see what *she* thought. She had been standing there not saying a word and with motherly worry on her face. She had probably said a few things before I came to.

"You boys better come in to supper," she said to Dad and me, then surprised me by just turning and picking up Charlotte Ann and carrying her on her way toward "Theodore Collins" on our mailbox on the other side of the road.

A few half minutes later, when I went past the mailbox myself on the way to the house to get washed up for supper—which I could smell was raw-fried potatoes, for sure—I stopped to look at the Collins name. With Dad beside me, it seemed that maybe as long as that name was on the mailbox, everything would be all right as long as a boy lived—if he could manage to live, with all the troubles he accidentally stumbled into.

"Hurry up, you two!" Mom called.

And we hurried.

6

The next day was a quiet sort of day with nothing very important happening except that Shorty's mother called up on the phone. I happened to answer it, since Mom was outdoors at the time.

"Is this Mrs. Collins?" a woman's cracking voice asked.

It sounded like Poetry's ducklike voice trying to be mischievous, so I said, "Yes, it is."

The voice became a little louder then. "This is Mrs. Long. We just wanted to call and tell you how much we appreciate your boy's carrying fresh water to our cow every day. I didn't know until last night that she wouldn't go to the spring. She's been so nervous ever since her calf got run over and killed the week before we moved. She's been afraid of her shadow. You know how you'd feel if you lost your only calf—I mean if you lost your only child—"

It still sounded like Poetry, so I cut in on the voice, saying, "Don't try to be funny. I know who you are!"

"What's that? I didn't hear what you said."

And then I felt myself cringing, as if I was in the top of a tree and the limb I was on was cracking and about to break. That voice *wasn't*

Poetry's squawky voice but was actually some woman's voice! It *was* Mrs. Long's voice, Shorty's mother!

Was I ever glad she hadn't heard me say, "Don't try to be funny."

"I'll call my mother," I said to her and was going to run to the kitchen door to call Mom in from the garden, where I supposed she was.

But the voice on the phone said, "Yes, I'm his mother. And that's another thing I wanted to tell you—I'm so sorry about the fights, but you know how boys are. I do hope your son didn't get badly hurt. I just found out about it this morning. We like to be neighborly. We'll make it up to you some way—about watering the cow, I mean. And I'll give my boy a talking to about fighting so much."

I decided that if she was that hard of hearing, there wasn't any use to try to tell her I *wasn't* Mrs. Theodore Collins, so I said, "Thank you, Mrs. Long."

She answered, "Thank you, Mrs. Collins. My boy's not as bad as he seems sometimes. We lived in such a rough neighborhood before— that's one reason we were glad to come back to Sugar Creek, so he could have some Christian playmates—"

And then that voice on the other end of the line broke, and I could tell there were tears in it and also in her eyes. And, as Mom says sometimes about somebody that's unhappy, she probably had "tears in her heart" too.

"You come and see us sometime," Mrs. Long finished just before she hung up.

I went outdoors to tell Mom what I had just heard and said.

For some reason as I pushed open the screen door and went out onto the board walk that leads to the iron pitcher pump, in spite of the fact that I had been listening to something that was half sad, I had one of the most wonderful feelings I had ever had in my heart.

I quickly pumped the pump handle up and down several times, catching the water in a tin cup and drinking a little. Then I threw the rest of it over the horse trough into the puddle that nearly always was there, startling about seventeen white-and-yellow butterflies who had been in a little huddle around the puddle drinking. They flew up in about seventeen directions as they always do. Then I quickly hung the cup on its wire hook and raced toward the two-by-four crossbeam of the grape arbor.

I made a flying-squirrel leap, caught onto it with my calloused hands, strengthened my biceps by chinning myself seven times, then skinned the cat and swung myself up on top. Remembering I had seen our old red rooster stand on the top of it once and flap his wings and crow, I did the same thing, waving my arms, flapping them down against my overall legs, and lifting my head and crowing a long *"Roo-uh-uh-uh-oooooooooooo!"*

Mom, who was out at the chicken coops by the orchard fence, heard and saw me at the same time and yelled, *"Bill Collins! Get down from there this minute! You'll break your neck! What on earth are you thinking?"*

"It's a wonderful day!" I called back to her as I started to come down, being able to do it without breaking my neck.

Then I looked toward the fence where she was, and what to my wondering eyes should appear but old Bentcomb with her wings spread in a mother hen mood. She was saying a fussy *"Cluck, cluck, cluck"* to about a dozen of the cutest, white, fluffy baby chickens I ever saw.

It was a wonderful day! Absolutely wonderful, I thought as I went on out to congratulate old Bentcomb on hatching such a fine family.

Even though Shorty's mother appreciated what I had done, Shorty himself didn't. Word got around to the gang that he didn't at all appreciate my carrying water to his cow. He was telling different people, especially Dragonfly, that if we hadn't scared his cow all to smithereens that time he and Dragonfly led her down to the spring for her first drink—*led* her, mind you!—she wouldn't have been afraid to go down every day, and I wouldn't have had to carry water for her.

Also, he said, I had tried to ram a pitchfork into her! He'd seen it with his own eyes and had given me a licking within an inch of my life.

Then one day, when I took a pail of water

out to pour it into the tub under the elderberry bush, there wasn't any tub! Instead, there was an envelope tied to a branch of the bush. It said on it, "For Bill Collins. Do not open till Christmas!"

The tub was gone! Mom's old but good washtub!

Christmas is right now! I said to myself grimly and tore open the envelope. Even while I was opening it, I thought maybe it might be a note from Shorty's mother, and I was trying to hold my dirigible down. But it wasn't from her.

"We don't need your help any longer," the printed note said. "Babe is drinking spring water now!"

That was the first time I knew what he called his crazy cow.

Then, below the last word in the middle of the yellow page was a picture of a boy with a very homely face. It had little pencil marks like periods and zeros all over it, and printed below the picture were the words: "Picture of a red-haired boy who can't fight!"

Two other pictures were in my mind as I climbed over the fence. One of them was what I would probably see when I found Mom's washtub, and the other was what the spring would look like now that, for some reason, Shorty's cow had gotten so she wasn't afraid to go down to it and get her own drinking water.

I expected to find Mom's tub out in the woods somewhere all smashed to nothing, and at the spring there would be cow tracks all over the place, our nice wooden bench knocked over into the mud and trampled upon and very dirty, and our drinking cups scattered everywhere.

"Just wait till the gang hears about this!" I muttered to myself and clenched my teeth.

I decided not to go to the spring alone. There wasn't any sense in running the risk of having another fight with Shorty when there wasn't even one of the gang there to watch me lick him—or even to watch me get licked, whichever it would be.

Besides, there was a verse I remembered from the Bible that was part of a prayer. It said, "Do not lead us into temptation." And it seemed it wouldn't be right for me to lead myself into temptation to have another battle. I knew that if I got all stirred up again, I'd probably rush right in as I sometimes had done in the past.

So I sort of moseyed over toward Poetry's house to show him the note and to get his idea on what to do.

I met him halfway, on the way to my house.

After I'd shown Poetry the note and the homely picture of me and told him about the tub and the spring, he said, "If my bench is knocked over again, there'll be a fight that boy'll never forget! That guy's just my size!"

Poetry really looked savage when he said that.

"Let's spy out the land first," we agreed. We also agreed not to hurt the cow if we found her at the spring.

"She lost her calf in an automobile accident," I told him, "and she hasn't gotten over it yet."

"You see what he called her in his note?" Poetry asked.

And I said, "Yeah. Babe!"

"That means," Poetry answered, "that he's imagining himself to be Paul Bunyan and able to do anything. Paul Bunyan was a *giant*."

"An imaginary one," I reminded him as we passed the papaw bushes and moved cautiously on toward the path that leads from the big Sugar Creek bridge to the spring.

Getting close enough to be seen by anybody who might be near the place, we dropped down and crept slowly along from bush to bush, keeping a sharp lookout every second. It would have been fun if we had been pretending to be scouts sneaking up on an imaginary enemy camp. But this wasn't any fun. This wasn't pretend.

"That boy and his cow are honest-to-goodness people," I said into Poetry's ear. We were side by side on our stomachs at the time.

He scowled and answered, "They're honest-to-*no*-goodness, you mean."

And I grinned at what was almost a cute remark.

"*Sh!* Listen!" he whispered.

"*Sh!* Look!" I answered. Already I had seen something blue moving near the linden tree.

Poetry let out an exclamation, as I felt one shooting out of my mind. There was something blue near the linden tree all right, but it was a boy in blue overalls with a water pail in his hands. He was pouring water into something that looked like—

"That's Mom's washtub!" I exclaimed.

"It's Dragonfly!" Poetry whispered back.

And it was! Dragonfly, the spindle-legged member of our gang. The neat little guy that I had always liked so well. The one who became a Christian by receiving the Savior when he was sliding down the very sycamore tree Poetry and I were on our stomachs under that very minute. There he was. Shorty's pal. Carrying water for him!

And then I saw Shorty himself. He walked over to look down into the tub. Then he made a movement as if he was giving orders.

Dragonfly picked up the pail, which he had set down, and started toward the linden tree and the incline that led down to the spring.

We could see perfectly from where we were, yet couldn't be seen from where they were, unless one of them really tried hard to see us. They were out in the open, and we weren't.

And then I saw something that was like lighting the gas under Mom's teakettle. Pretty soon my temper would be to the boiling point. Shorty was standing there at the top of the incline, looking down to where Dragonfly had just gone. He had his elbows out and his fists on his hips, as much as to say, "I'm the boss around here!"

Poetry whispered in my ear then, saying, "He's making Dragonfly carry the water for him!"

For one second I had been looking down the side of my nose to see if I could see my upper lip. Also, I was flexing my biceps for some reason. When Poetry said that, it was like somebody had turned the gas a little higher under the teakettle.

"He thinks he's a big shot!" Poetry growled.

I saw Dragonfly's brown hair appear at the top of the slope, then he himself, struggling, carrying up the big two-and-one-half-gallon pail of water with both hands. Reaching the top, he set it down and stood panting for breath.

Shorty made a quick bossy move with his arms and gave a jerk of his head. I knew that if I could have heard his voice, I'd probably have heard him say, "Don't be such a wimp!" And then he lunged toward Dragonfly as if he was going to wham him with two of the hardest fists a boy could ever get whammed with.

Dragonfly ducked, flinging up his arms to protect himself, and stooped to pick up the heavy pail of water again.

It was maddening. Even though it actually wasn't any of our business, it looked as if it was. It was *my* mother's washtub. It was *our* spring-water. It was Dragonfly, who belonged to *our* gang, who was being bossed around by a bully.

And then I *did* see something that upset me. It was Dragonfly leaning over, and his chest was heaving, and he was also coughing.

"He's got his asthma!" I cried under my breath.

How many times I had seen that little guy get behind in his breathing because some pollen that was poisonous to him had made his bronchial tubes swell and he couldn't get air in or out without having to fight for practically every breath he took. *Poor little guy!* I thought.

"The big bully!" Poetry muttered. He shuffled to his feet, getting there a few seconds after I did.

With our jaws set and our minds made up, we stepped out into the open, and I heard myself yelling, "You great big bully!"

We started on the run toward the tub and the water pail and our pal Dragonfly, whose thin chest had hard enough work to keep him in air when he was just doing what a boy did naturally. It wasn't enough to supply him when he had to carry a big pail of water up a steep hill.

We were also on our way toward one of the fiercest fighters around, one with the dirtiest mind a boy ever had, and one who thought he was a big shot.

Even as we ran, I was remembering that Bible verse about being led into temptation. I realized this wasn't any temptation to do something *wrong*. Instead, I was going to help a little guy who could hardly breathe and was being bullied by a big lummox almost twice his size.

Even though Dragonfly had made his choice and had been on Shorty's side for weeks, I was making *my* choice now. I was going to rescue that little allergic-nosed member of the Sugar Creek Gang from a dangerous situation.

In another short minute we would be there. That is, we *would* have been, but we had to dodge around a brush pile beside a thicket of hazelnut bushes. And just as I swung out to miss it, a four-legged mammal with horns swung out of those bushes into my path.

I ran *ker-wham* into her fast-moving blue side and got bowled over as if I had been struck with the side of a barn. I landed sprawling in the middle of a patch of mayapples. My tongue somehow got between my teeth while I was falling. My teeth closed on it, and I got a bad bite on the right side of my tongue. I'd had that kind of bite before, and once I could hardly talk for almost a day.

I was up again in a jiffy, but Shorty had seen me wham into his cow and seen me get bowled over and land sprawling in the mayapples. He started to laugh, saying, "Goody, goody, goody! The goody-goody boy got his goody-goody head bumped!"

Now, I ask you, what would *you* have done?

But you weren't there, were you? Besides, I had to make up my own mind—what little I had at the time.

One thing I wasn't going to do—I wasn't going to rush into a temper-bloated fight with a skillful boxer such as Shorty had proved to me he was. Besides, I'd licked him once in a one-sock fight, and it hadn't done him a bit of good. Not even a little bit.

But I couldn't decide for Poetry. Besides, he hadn't had *his* fight with Shorty yet. And if ever a boy was mad at anything, it was Poetry when he thought somebody was being bullied.

I yelled for him to stop a minute, while I was getting myself out of the mayapple patch. I expected to see him charge like a bull straight for Shorty Long.

But Poetry had more presence of mind than I thought. When he got to within about fifteen feet of Shorty, he stopped, and I stopped beside him. The two of us glared at the one of him, and he glared back at us, while Dragonfly was leaning against the linden tree and still breathing hard. Lugging that heavy pail of water up that hill had been too much for him.

And then I saw the savage-looking knife in Shorty's hand and the smoldering look in his eyes as he stood beside his water pail. The tub was right behind him and also the rope he used at different times to lead or try to lead his cow to water or to the corral for milking.

It seemed I was letting Poetry be the leader just then, especially when he called out, "You've made a slave out of Roy Gilbert long enough! You're going to release him now! Come on, Dragonfly! You're coming with us!"

That little guy was still struggling for breath. "I–I can't. I–can't walk–yet." And he kept on struggling to breathe. He started to come toward us, though.

But he got stopped by his big boss thundering back at him, *"Stop!"*

Dragonfly stopped, but I saw him make a quick little jerk of his head, and I noticed that he was breathing harder than ever, struggling and panting and acting so helpless that Shorty needn't have worried about his trying to get away. I'd seen him fighting for breath many times, but never had he worked as hard as that.

I knew now was the time. I'd have to run the risk of being able to dodge the knife, which that bully was probably dumb enough to actually use if we attacked him. But I thought I could do it.

Like a charging football lineman, I started toward Shorty and Dragonfly, who was behind him and still panting.

"Back there! You get back!" I shook both my fists and shouted fiercely. *"Back, you lummox!"*

Just that second Dragonfly dropped to the ground.

And just that second Shorty did step back—or started to. But his heels bumped into a boy who for some reason was on his hands and knees right behind him. Shorty lost his balance and leaned sideways to try to regain it. The boy behind him grabbed him around the knees and one second later by the wrist of the hand that had the knife in it and—

That Dragonfly was a wiry little guy. He was fighting like a tiger, holding onto the knife hand and butting Shorty in the stomach with his head even before Poetry and I could get there, which I tell you we really did in a thundering hurry.

"Quick!" Dragonfly exclaimed. "The rope, over there by the linden tree! Get it!"

And we got it!

In less than four minutes—my powerful biceps helping quite a lot—we made short work of Shorty Long. We got both his hands and his feet tied and stretched him out on the ground on the closely cropped bluegrass by the Black Widow Stump. The grass there had been eaten down to the ground by Paul Bunyan's blue cow.

I was still panting and getting my breath from having worked so hard so fast, and so was Poetry. But Dragonfly—he was breathing normally! Not even as hard as we were!

"Hey!" I said to him. "You haven't got the asthma anymore! The excitement was good for you. It waked up your adrenalin glands."

"Who said anybody had the asthma?" that little guy said disdainfully.

"But you were panting for breath! You could hardly live five minutes ago!"

"I don't get asthma till the ragweeds come. This is still the last of May."

I looked at his grinning face, and he looked back at me, then up at the sky with an indifferent expression as much as to say, "I thought that would be a good way to get myself saved. I got tired of doing all his hard work for nothing." Then his face took on a mussed-up look, and I knew he was going to sneeze, which right away he did—a nice long-tailed sneeze that could have been heard a long ways away.

"I guess I'm allergic to cow's hair a little bit! Is there a cow around here somewhere?" And I could tell by the happy grin on his face that he had come back into our gang and was going to be one of us the rest of the summer and all his life.

"You *tricked* me!" Shorty growled from where he was lying over by Babe's drinking water. "I'll make you pay for it, you little crooked-nosed scalawag!"

I boiled at that. *I* could call Dragonfly a crooked-nosed boy when I was talking about him or writing it in a story, but I had never said it in any way that would be an insult.

But Shorty was helpless there in spite of his grunting and squirming and swearing, so I couldn't condescend to do anything to hurt him.

But we did have to decide what to do with him—and whether or not to punish him. And if we punished him, what kind of punishment would it be?

What kind did he deserve?

It was Big Jim who helped us decide. He all of a sudden came over the brow of the hill from the direction of my house to ask us about something that was even more important.

I heard him coming before I saw him and also before I saw Little Jim, the very littlest member of the gang, running along beside him like a small spring lamb in a pasture. Seeing that cute little fellow with his innocent face always makes me feel fine. It also makes me feel kinder toward anybody I'm having trouble with. So I was glad he had come along, because he usually didn't have as much trouble with his attitudes as I did.

Just then there was an earsplitting screaming yell from near Babe's tub of drinking water. "Help! They're torturing me!" Shorty's voice was wild enough and loud enough to have been heard three town blocks away.

And then I heard an answer from away up along the bayou! "Where are you?"

"Down by the spring! Hurry!" Shorty's voice sounded as if he was being half killed.

I looked in the direction of the bayou, where I knew the robin family now had a cute little family of baby robins in their nest. And right that second there was a neighborhood uproar of robins' voices and thrushes' voices, scolding.

And then I saw a round man waddling toward us.

"It's Shorty's dad!" Dragonfly cried, and his face was afraid again. "What'll we do now?"

7

I'd seen Shorty's two-hundred-twenty-five-pound father quite a few times since they had moved into our neighborhood that spring and also when they had lived here before. But I had never felt I knew him very well. He always had been very busy, or his mind seemed he was thinking about somebody or someplace far away, even when he was within only a few feet of me. It always seemed he was thinking about something more important than what any of us were doing or saying.

The path Mr. Long was walking on had taken him behind two or three evergreens. "Look at that fancy shirt!" Poetry whispered to me as the two-hundred-or-so pounds came into sight again.

The sport shirt he was wearing was a bright gold color with purple grapes all over it, but the thing I noticed when he got up close was his mustache. It was certainly a sporty one, too small for such a broad face, and because he kind of strutted when he walked, the mustache made him look like a sissy. But the fierce-looking beech switch he was carrying made him look dangerous.

I don't know what happened to Shorty's mind during the few minutes between the time when he had called for help and when he saw his father with the beech switch coming down the path and into the open space where we were. But he took one look at the switch and right away was a different boy, as if he was scared of his shadow.

"What have you been doing all morning, Guenther?" his father thundered. "Don't you ever stop to think your mother might need a little help?"

He stomped over to where his boy was all tied up, looked down at him, scowling, and demanded, "Now you get yourself untied and get home and get busy in the garden! Do you *hear* me?"

Then that heavy body of Shorty's father swung around, and I felt his beady eyes boring into me and into all of us. "Don't you boys ever do anything but waste your time playing cops and robbers? Let's see you get those ropes off my son, and be quick about it! I'd think you could all find a little something to do at home! How do you expect my boy to amount to anything—playing around with a gang of loafers!"

For some reason I was having trouble with my attitude again, and I thought that there were enough of us boys with strong enough muscles to make short work of Shorty's father too. Dragonfly could plop down behind him, one of us could give him a powerful shove, and, when he landed on the ground, the rest of us could pile all over him and teach him how to be courteous in one easy lesson.

It wasn't a good idea. Anyway, Big Jim didn't seem to think so.

I remembered that Big Jim hadn't been with us when Poetry and Dragonfly and I had had our scuffle with Guenther Long—what a name for a boy to have! And he hadn't seen Dragonfly struggle up the hill with the heavy pail of water, either, nor had he read the insulting note that had been tied to the elderberry bush, or anything. He must have thought we *were* really playing some kind of game and had just tied Shorty up—and when he had screamed for help a few minutes ago, he was just pretending, the way boys do in their games.

Big Jim's words came out very politely from under his almost mustache: "You're right, Mr. Long. We *do* have work at home. But our parents arrange for us to have time to play together, too. We try to cooperate with our parents, and they try to cooperate with the gang."

Mr. Long whirled and shot back at Big Jim, "Wise guy, eh? You think I don't cooperate with my son? Well, I would have you know my son doesn't cooperate with his parents! The essence of cooperation is obedience, unquestioning obedience! Now you get those ropes off my boy! I've got to leave for the city in fifteen minutes, and I want him home before I go!"

If Big Jim had known what I knew, and if he had had my mind and my attitude, he would probably have said, "Untie him yourself. It's your rope, it's your good-for-nothing son, who probably got his ideas and disposition from his father, and we're not moving a muscle. Not even one!" Then he would have ordered our gang to walk off and leave those two just-alike people to look after themselves.

Instead, Big Jim was satisfied just to let the muscles of his jaw work as he said to Mr. Long, "Certainly. I'm sure we didn't realize the situation. We're glad to cooperate."

He walked over to where Shorty was lying and began to untie the extrahard knots I myself had tied only a few minutes before. I, with my own jaw muscles working and my teeth pressed tight together, hurried over to help him. Poetry sat on the grass with a set face and smoldering eyes and watched.

Little Jim was on his knees, grunting away on one of the knots, while Dragonfly stood and looked on, holding his nose as if he was trying to stop a sneeze. He probably wasn't but was holding it for another reason, which was that the whole thing "smelled."

As soon as Guenther was free, he rolled to his feet, took a quick look at his father and the heavy switch he had in his hand, and started on the run up the bayou path, not even saying good-bye.

And, without a word, the fancy gold-and-purple sport shirt with a man in it followed him.

I let my mind follow them a lot farther than my eyes could see, as Big Jim, Little Jim, Poetry, Dragonfly, and I started up another path through the woods toward home to see if maybe there *was* something our parents needed us for. All the way, while we explained everything to the two Jims, from the note on the elderberry bush to the washtub at the spring, I was still following with my mind's eye that small neatly trimmed mustache and the gaudy shirt.

It kind of seemed it wasn't important anymore whether I ever grew a mustache myself or not. I guess I really didn't want to *wear* one, anyway. I just wanted to be big enough to grow one so that I could have my first shave.

That night while Dad and I were doing the chores, he and I happened to be in the haymow at the same time. While I was throwing down quite a few forkfuls of alfalfa, he was looking around, studying the layout of the floor. Then he picked up the basketball that had been lying there and tossed a few baskets, actually hitting several while I worked. It made me grin, because I didn't expect him to be that good.

"You ought to belong to our team," I said. "How come you're so good?"

"Played on a college team once," he said.

I answered, "Is that so?"

He knew I knew it was so. I'd heard him tell about it many a time when he and Mom were visiting with some other man and his wife. Dad always liked to say, "That's where I met *Mrs.* Collins. She saw me playing, and—"

It was an old joke about Mom's liking his

basketball playing so well that she wanted him to take her home that night. "And then, after a few dates," Dad always wound up by saying, "she liked my playing so well that she asked me to take her to my home. And I've had her ever since—and I've been *working* ever since."

Mom, being smart, always says, "That's right."

Dad made another basket, then he called me over and said, "Want to shoot a few before we have to close up the court for the summer?"

I had the ball almost before he had finished saying that. But when I realized *what* he had said, I stopped, with the ball poised in my two hands.

"Maybe we can fix up a basket out on the north side of the barn so you can keep in practice. But the ladino hay's going to have to have a place up here somewhere, and it'll be ready to cut next week. I thought you'd like to know about it."

It was a kind of shock to realize that I was going to have my basketball court all covered with five or six feet of new hay, but I said, "Sure, that'll be OK. It's kind of hot up here in the summertime. It'll be cooler outdoors in the shade of the barn, anyway."

Then I took careful aim and shot at the basket, while in my mind's eye I was a college student, and a whole crowd of other college kids was watching a game. And one of the girls watching was the one who was the cause of my knocking the living daylights out of Shorty for saying something bad about her.

I didn't do so well with my baskets, though.

Dad threw down another forkful of hay and said, "Well, let's get going. That's a nice song you're whistling."

I didn't know I had been whistling anything at all, but I listened to myself to see if I was, and sure enough I had been. The words of the song were ones we had on a record we sometimes played on our record player. They were chasing themselves up and down the scale in my mind and were:

> *I want a girl just like the girl*
> *That married dear old Dad . . .*

"Can you come here a minute, Son?" Dad called from the ladder that led to the downstairs of the barn.

When I got there, just before either one of us started to put a foot on the top rung and go down, Dad put an arm across my shoulder and said, "Bill, your whistling that song reminded me of something I've been wanting to say and sort of waiting for a chance that would be just right before doing it. You know what the words are, don't you?"

"Yes sir," I answered, feeling his arm across my shoulder and wondering if maybe he had heard about Shorty and he was going to give me some advice of some kind.

Then he said in a confidential tone like the one Poetry uses when he is telling me a secret, "You're probably a little young to be thinking about things like this. But someday you will, and when you do, keep your mother's fine high ideals in mind, will you? And her faith in God?"

It's a good thing I wasn't halfway down the ladder at the time, because somehow I couldn't see straight for some crazy old tears that had gotten into my eyes. The haymow and the opening that the top of the ladder was braced against were all blurred.

"I will," I said to Dad, having to say it twice because I had sort of lost my voice.

I slipped out from under his arm then, and he went on down the ladder while I took just one more shot at the basket, taking careful aim first. The brown ball arched up in a high curve and whisked down right through the center of the net without even touching the rim.

I had a pretty wonderful mother, I thought, as I dived into the chores, working faster and harder than I had in a long time. It seemed easy to cooperate with Dad, and his having a reddish brown mustache didn't make a bit of difference. I might even grow one myself some-day. In fact, I might even let it keep on growing and not shave it off.

One day soon after that, in fact just two days before Dad's mowing machine went singing round and round the field cutting the ladino clover, I had my worst experience with an imaginary Paul Bunyan and his honest-to-no-goodness blue cow.

Dad had to go to the city on business of

some kind and would have to stay all night—
there was some kind of Farm Bureau meeting.
He would drive back the next day. Just to be
friendly with Mr. Long, Dad offered to take
him along with him if he had any business in
the city, and Mr. Long did.

It would be my job to be the man of the
house, Dad said, and "look after the stock and
your mother and your kid sister. Protect them
from wolves, and don't leave any gates open,
and gather the eggs and feed the chickens, and
give Old Addie some nice fresh straw, and if
you have any time left, see if Mother may need
a little help around the house."

"Yes sir," I answered and saluted him. He
was in the car at the time, and Mom was standing with Charlotte Ann on her arm beside the
left front door. I heard her say, "Now *do* drive
carefully, Dad."

"Sure, sure, sure, sure, sure, sure," Dad said
and gave us all a final good-bye, saying to Mom
as he drove away—I heard it and probably
wasn't supposed to—"I left a note for you in
the egg basket. It may not seem important, but
you might want to read it." Then he was off,
and the car swished past the mailbox on the
way to Guenther Long's father's house to pick
him up.

I forgot all about the note Dad had said
he'd left for Mom in the egg basket. I never
thought about it again until that night about
nine o'clock, when I was upstairs just about
ready to turn out the light and tumble into

bed. Then I got to thinking: maybe Dad had written something on it for *me*. In fact, maybe he had meant it for both of us, and Mom had forgotten about it. Maybe there was something special he wanted done around the place that he wouldn't like if I didn't do it.

I stood looking out in the moonlight, the way I nearly always do just before I drop down on my knees for a short prayer and before giving up the wonderful day I nearly always have had and forgetting about it while I wait asleep for the next one.

Thinking about the note in the basket and wondering if it might have been meant for me too—Mom hadn't given me any extra orders— I stepped into my overalls and crept stealthily along the banister to the stairs and down them. With my flashlight I moved quietly into the kitchen so as not to waken Mom and Charlotte Ann. They were in the bedroom away on the other side of the living room and wouldn't hear me unless I stumbled over something.

I shined my light into the egg basket that always stands on a table by the east window, which I noticed was open. If it rained during the night, I must be sure to rush down and close it. I mustn't forget anything. So far I hadn't. All the chores had been done as nearly exactly right as I could do them, and I deserved a good night's sleep.

But there wasn't any piece of paper or envelope in the egg basket, so I decided Mom had gotten it and that what had been on it was for her only and not for me. I was about to go back to my upstairs room when I spied some pencil writing on one of the white eggs.

I picked up the egg, and Dad had written all around it, starting at the top and writing round and round and round.

Well, it wasn't any of my business at all, I found out. As quickly and as quietly as I could, I put the egg back, and, because the back door was standing open, I decided to see if the screen door was hooked, just for sure, and it was. Then, seeing the iron pitcher pump out at the end of the moonlit board walk, I unhooked the screen door to go out to get a drink.

"Is that you, Bill?" Mom called from the other room.

I called back, "I'm thirsty. You want a drink, too?"

"Why, yes, I believe I do," she called. "It's a pretty hot night."

I took her a drink, and, while she was sitting up in bed drinking it in the light of my flashlight, I remembered the note in the basket and said, "I heard Dad say he had left a note for you in the egg basket. It might be important."

"I've already read it," she said, handing me the empty cup.

As I started to carry it back to the kitchen and on out to the pump to hang it on the wire hook there, she said, "That was very thoughtful of you, Bill. Thank you again—and good night! You're getting to be more and more like your father in little things like that."

As soon as I had the cup on the wire hook, I was ready to go in and back to bed. But I didn't get to go for a few minutes, because I heard a noise up the road in the direction of the corral where, every morning and night, Shorty or his father or both of them managed to get their blue cow penned up so they could milk her— she never wanted to be milked and never wanted to be corralled.

I shined my light up the road to see if I could see anything. I couldn't, but I knew I had heard something. Well, as "the man of the house" and of the barn, and feeling fine because I was thoughtful about little things like my father, I took a quick hike up the gravel road to see if old Babe was there, or near there, and was all right. She sometimes stayed in the corral, with its open gate on the woods side, until morning. Then, when they came to milk her, she'd make a dive for the opening and have to be rounded up again.

I found her there, and all right, lying on her side and chewing her cud. The only thing was, this time she was penned up and couldn't get out. I shined the light on her, and her eyes looked pretty scared, but she didn't start to run wild or anything.

So I said to her, "That's what you deserve. They get tired of having to chase you down every morning. You'll be right here when Guenther comes in the morning to milk you."

I left her and went on back down the road to the house, feeling happy inside that I had gone to look after the cow. I guess I was happy because of something else too. Even though I wasn't supposed to have read what Dad had written on the egg, I knew I would never forget it.

The words went round and round in my mind as I undressed again, turned out the light, and went to bed. By this time Dad would be over a hundred miles away in the big city, and he would probably go to sleep with a grin on his face as he remembered what he had written to Mom:

> I won't have a chance to tell you straight out that I think you're a wonderful wife and mother, so I take this roundabout way of saying, *I love you.*

The note had been signed: "Your bum husband, Theo."

I grinned to myself as I remembered it, and then I sighed a great big sigh, thinking about all my responsibilities tomorrow. I dropped off to sleep, not knowing that one of tomorrow's responsibilities was going to start early in the morning, and that, before nine o'clock, I'd have wished a thousand times that Dad had been home to help me save Paul Bunyan's blue cow's life from having eaten too much fresh dew-wet ladino clover on an empty stomach. Her stomach was empty before she started to eat because she had emptied it out by chewing her cud all night and swallowing it back into

her other stomach. And she had been in the
corral all night and had not gotten to eat even
one bite of bluegrass or other cow food that
grew in the woods.

8

I had the chores almost finished the next morning and was just winding up the milking, sitting on Dad's metal, twelve-inch-high, three-legged milk stool, stripping old Jersey Jill, my favorite cow friend. She was always as gentle and easy to manage as Guenther Long's Babe was cantankerous.

I was making the last few strokes to get the rich, creamy milk out of her udder and feeling fine because I had looked after Mom and Charlotte Ann and the stock and everything. I didn't know that a few minutes later there'd be an excited interruption that would knock all the peace of mind out of me.

"Just sixteen more squeezes, and I'll be through," I said to Jersey Jill.

She was acting a little impatient, as much as to say, "I wish you'd keep your fingernails trimmed a little better! That hurts like everything!" She switched her tail at me a few times, as though I was as much a nuisance as a dozen flies buzzing around. She also lifted her right hind foot several times, as if she would like to set it down in the pail if she could.

So I said, *"So!"* which any farm boy knows means, "Stop whatever you're doing!"

Mixy was meowing hungrily and moving

faster and faster around my legs and arching her back and rubbing her sides against Jersey Jill's front legs and acting impatient herself. So I quickly took a few last short strokes, getting practically nothing more in the pail, and the milking was done.

"That's it!" I said to Jersey Jill. "Now you wait right here till I get this milk up to the house, and I'll be back to turn you out to pasture."

I was on my feet, the milk pail in one hand and the three-legged stool in the other, starting toward the cattle-shed door, when I heard a boy's voice calling.

"Swo-o-ok! Swo-o-o-k!"

I knew it was Shorty somewhere out in the woods across the road, calling his cow. I'd heard him call her many times the past month, ever since Babe had been living there. I felt sorry for Shorty, because he probably had never known how nice it was to have a well-trained cow like Jersey Jill.

And then I thought, *How come he's calling her? She was in the corral all night, just like I'd had Jersey Jill in her corral on the south side of our barn.*

I hung up the milk stool in its place and stepped outside to look toward the woods to see where Guenther was. I was thinking that as soon as I had the milk carried to the house and Jersey Jill in her own pasture east of the barn, I'd run out and help him round up his cow. Maybe Babe had gotten out and was down along the bayou somewhere, not wanting to be milked.

I could save time, I thought, if I'd let Jersey Jill out right now and let her run up to her trough at the pitcher pump. She could be drinking while I went on into the house with the milk.

The idea seemed to exactly suit my contented cow. The very second she was out in the bright sunlight, she started on the run for her drink as though I had forgotten to water her last night, which I hoped I hadn't.

I stopped as Dad always does and poured a little fresh milk into Mixy's breakfast bowl on the barn floor beside the cabinet where Dad kept his shelf of farm library books and all his special tools and medicines for the stock.

When I got to the iron pitcher pump a minute or two later, Jersey Jill was busy helping herself. "I'll be back in a minute," I said to her. She looked up at me with a question mark in her brown eyes as Shorty Long's voice called from across the road near the elderberry bushes, saying, *"Swo-o-o-o-ok! Swo-o-o-o-ok!"*

"I'll be over and help you round her up in a few minutes," I called.

He called back, "I can't find her anywhere."

Mom, I was glad to notice, was just wiping the last breakfast dish when I reached the kitchen door. She said, "What's all the excitement about?"

"Paul Bunyan's cow again," I answered. "He can't find her. I promised him I'd help."

"That's thoughtful of you," Mom said.

I thought so myself—after all the things Shorty had done to me—but I didn't say so.

I set the heavy pail on the worktable where Mom wanted it and went back outdoors to drive Jersey Jill, my good-mannered, well-trained cow to her own mostly bluegrass pasture, which was only about one-sixth clover and was safest for cows. It also was good for cows to eat some *dry* food if there was a lot of clover or alfalfa in their pasture, so there wouldn't be so much gas formed in their paunches.

But even nice-mannered cows sometimes get mischievous streaks and take a notion they don't want to do what you want them to do. All of a sudden, old Jersey Jill started off in another direction, heading toward the pignut trees away up on the other side of our garden.

"Oh, no, you don't!" I exclaimed and was after her like a shot. I grabbed up an ash stick I had carried home from the bayou yesterday and started on the run to head her off. I had used part of the stick to make a new arrow, and this was what was left.

Seeing the stick, Jersey Jill broke into a run ahead of me, making the straightest cow path you ever saw in the direction of the pignut trees.

Oh well, I thought, why waste good breath, when Dad and I had made a good fence and put it along the side of the clover field? She'd stop when she got to the new gate that was hanging on the big cedar post my powerful biceps had dug a hole for that spring.

But old Jersey Jill didn't stop at the gate! And why? Because, to my astonishment, the gate was *open,* and she went swishing through and right out into that clover field. She stopped quick after she was about fifteen feet out in it. Dropping her hornless head into the rich, green, all-clover pasture, she started eating as though she hadn't had anything so wonderful in her diet in a long time.

Well, there are a lot of things around a farm that stir up a boy's temper a little, and something like that was one of them. I quickened my pace to a fast run, reached the pignut trees in a few seconds, and zipped through the new no-sag gate myself, wondering how it had gotten open in the first place.

Waving my ash stick, I swung out into the field to make a wide arc around her so that I could drive her back out and shut the gate and get her into her own safe pasture.

"I hope you realize, young lady," I called to her, "that people get punished for things like this! Just because a *blue* cow goes on a rampage is no reason why a fawn-colored one can do it!"

She kept on taking great big hungry swipes at the clover with her rough tongue, biting off mouthfuls and swallowing them fast, ignoring me except to sidle away and eat as she went, running only a few feet and getting another mouthful. I knew she wasn't chewing it. She'd wait till later, as cows do, and then she'd lie down somewhere or maybe find a shade tree and stand with a contented expression on her face and swallow the food backward, one mouthful at a time, and chew it, and swallow it all over again into her *second* stomach. And no matter what color her food had been, she would digest it and make it into white milk.

The only thing was, she wasn't headed toward the gate but toward the bottom of the hill, down by the other iron pitcher pump we had away down there for watering our stock when we had them in this field.

And then I saw something that made me feel goose bumps all over. For down by the fence—in knee-deep clover, not eating but just standing and gasping for breath, her sides bulging, looking like a big blue balloon with four legs under it—was Shorty's blue cow with the *bloat!*

She was panting and groaning as she struggled for breath.

And now, what was I, the head of the house, taking my father's place, going to do? One thing I remembered from *What to Do Before the Doctor Arrives* was the need to chase the cow up a hill, keep her moving, not let her stop and lie down, or it'd be forever too late. Also, "Phone for the veterinarian *quick!*"

I knew old Jersey Jill couldn't eat enough in only a few minutes to get the bloat, so I'd have to let *her* go and try to save Shorty's cow. Her case was an emergency.

I started yelling for Mom as loud as I could as I ran for the top of the hill to where she could see and hear me.

She heard me all right. She was out on the back steps when I got to where she could see me, and she called, "What's the matter? You're making enough noise to wake up the whole neighborhood."

"The whole neighborhood needs to be waked up!" I yelled back. "Old Babe Bunyan's got the *bloat!* She's out in the clover field with the *bloat!* Call the veterinarian!"

"Where is she?" Mom called.

"Out in our clover field, down by the pump! She's gasping for breath harder than I am! She's bigger than the side of a barn!"

And then is when I found out something about Mom I never knew before. Boy oh boy, she flew into action faster than an old setting hen can go racing across the barnyard when she's just been let off the nest.

She shot orders back to me like lightning. "I'll phone him! You race out to the barn for the funnel and an empty pint bottle out of the cabinet, and bring them here. *Hurry!* We'll have to drench her!"

It was just like an army that was about to lose a battle all of a sudden getting a new captain that knew what to do.

And I hurried. In less than two shakes of a lamb's tail I was in the barn, found the bottle right where it was handy, grabbed up the funnel that was there just as though somebody had placed it there on purpose, which Dad probably had, and went racing to the house with it.

Mom took it quick and ordered me, "Run

back to the pasture and keep her moving. Don't let her stop or lie down. Drive her uphill—always *up*hill, so her head will be higher than her body. We've got to get her to start belching!"

"I will," I said, glad I had taken time that spring to read what to do in case a cow gets the bloat.

Even as I ran toward the open gate, where Jersey Jill lifted her head and stared at me head-on, I got a glimpse of Mom's fast-flying blue apron with her behind it, rushing to the shelf beside the toolshed and pouring kerosene into the bottle through the funnel.

I reached the gate, dodged around Jersey Jill, who for some crazy reason just stood there in the way, and ran on with my ash stick toward the four-legged blue balloon that was staggering around, trying to keep from falling down. She was gasping and looking bleary-eyed.

She's dying! I thought and wondered who would be to blame. Had I accidentally left our gate open myself yesterday when I'd gone through to look for my new arrow? I suddenly sadly remembered I had missed what I had been shooting at and my straight ash arrow had gone far out into this very field!

It wouldn't matter who had been to blame for Babe's getting out of the woods, which probably was herself, but if I had left *this* gate open—

That thought was too sad. I hoped the veterinarian would hurry up and come—really hurry. And I hoped Mom and I could keep Babe alive till he got here.

"Hey!" I cried to old Babe when I got near her. If only she would get scared and start on a wild run for the gate *up the hill!*

But she didn't. She *couldn't!* That I found out after a few seconds of shouting and using the ash stick on her. I didn't want to hurt her, but I knew I *had* to sock her and make her keep moving so that she could belch and get the gas up and out and her life saved.

After a lot of pushing and coaxing and scolding and whipping, she did start to move awkwardly in the direction I was trying to get her to go.

I had even begun to feel a little encouraged when all of a sudden I heard Shorty's angry voice calling down to me from the pignut trees. He was yelling and saying, "You leave my cow alone! Don't you dare hit her with that big club!"

"I'm trying to save her life!" I yelled back up to him. "She's dying, and if we can't get her to belch, she'll be dead in thirty minutes if the veterinarian doesn't get here!"

And I started whamming his cow on the rump again and demanding she get going. "Uphill!" I yelled to her. "You've got to run uphill to save your life! You've got to belch that gas up! Keep your head higher than your body!"

I don't suppose I ought to have blamed Shorty for not understanding, because what would *he* know about what to do before the doctor came? Seeing me whamming away on his cow with my ash stick, he lost his temper and started on the run for me, yelling angrily, "This time I'll *really* knock you out!"

I took my eyes off his cow for just long enough to read the temper in his eyes and face, and I knew that I'd have to do something I didn't want to do. If he got me into a fight and kept me from keeping his cow on the move, or if he really knocked me out as he said he was going to do, he'd have a dead cow on his hands.

It seemed I needed help from somebody to decide what to do. I'd had my mind made up that I'd never fight that boy again, and I'd made a promise to myself that I wouldn't. Also I'd asked Somebody Else to help me keep from it, and He had up to now.

Was I going to fight Shorty, dive into him when he wasn't looking, and land a one-sock punch on the same jaw I'd socked once before and knocked him out with it? Or let him knock me out? Or while we were fighting, let his cow die?

If only Mom would hurry up with the bottle of kerosene and milk so we could drench her. A little kerosene and milk poured down her throat might get her started to belch, and she'd be saved—till the vet came, anyway. If he could *only* get here in time!

I didn't even have time to say a prayer, but I thought one of the quickest ones I had ever thought in my life. And almost in a flash of a second it seemed I had an answer. What He made me think of was: *Pretend to be a coward. Pretend to be afraid! Keep running round and round the cow. And every time you circle her, sock her and dodge Shorty's fists, and we'll keep her on the move.*

"Don't you *dare* hurt me!" I cried to Shorty in a tearful voice. "Don't you dare!"

And I started to run in circles around his cow, hitting her when I had a chance and using a crying voice as I begged him not to hurt me. I whacked his cow just enough to keep him mad at me, and all the time she was moving and getting nearer the top of the hill. And also all the time I was wishing Mom would come, and she didn't. I was wishing the vet would come, and *he* didn't.

"You coward!" Shorty cried. He kept lunging for me.

And then I stumbled and fell.

In a flash he was on top of me and whamming away. And that's where I changed from a scaredy-cat into a tiger. In a second I was fighting back, with all my savage temper boiling. And at the same time I think I must have been praying too, not wanting to really injure Shorty but to hurt him just enough so that I could get to my feet and keep on saving his cow.

"You can take *that*—and *that*—and *that!*" I said.

And all of a sudden he started to cry and to beg me to stop, which I was glad to do.

I got to my feet as quick as I could, just as Mom got there with the pint bottle of chalky-looking drenching medicine. "There wasn't enough kerosene in the can," she said. "I had to find some."

Boy oh boy, my mother was better than any veterinarian could ever have been. Some girls are scared of even an innocent fishing worm, but Mom wasn't any more a helpless woman than the man in the moon.

In no time at all she had her thumb and the first two fingers of her left hand in Babe's nostrils. Then she was lifting the cow's head and pushing the neck of the pint bottle into the side of her mouth. She poured the mixture of kerosene and fresh milk right down Shorty's cow's throat.

In a minute now, I thought, *if it's going to work, she'll start to belch, and she'll be saved.*

Behind us, Shorty cried, "What are you trying to do to her? What are you *giving* her?"

"Kerosene!" I answered. "We're trying to save her!"

"Kerosene!" he exclaimed angrily. "That'll *kill* her!"

But it didn't. Also, it didn't seem to help her a bit.

Mom, who had been as cool as a veterinarian up to now, suddenly seemed worried. "It's not doing any good. Look at her—she's gasping for her very life! We'll have to *tap* her. It's our only chance." She turned to Shorty. "Here, Guenther!"

And Shorty, seeing Babe gasping and panting a thousand times worse than Dragonfly had panted and gasped that other day leaning against the linden tree, seemed to finally believe that we were really trying to help.

"Hold her halter a minute while I try to get a little more down her throat. Bill, you run down to the cabinet for the trocar. We'll have to tap her!"

"The *trocar*?" I asked and frowned. "What's that?"

"Don't ask questions. Go get it. It's a stylet. You know. Didn't you ever see it in the cabinet? There by the iodine. Bring the iodine too!"

A sickening sensation came over me. "Does it have a round smooth handle and a triangle-pointed tip?"

"That's it—now *hurry!*"

I hurried, but I didn't run toward the barn. I ran toward the toolshed, where I'd had the thing only yesterday, using it to make a triangular design on a piece of leather.

"Not *that* way! To the *barn*! In the *cabinet*!" Mom called.

But I yelled back over my shoulder, "I saw it in the toolshed yesterday," and away I went.

At the toolshed I stumbled over the empty kerosene can lying there and yanked open the toolshed door, which I was glad I had forgotten to close and lock last night. And in a second I was on my way to the barn for the iodine.

I found it right where I remembered it to be and went out the door, again up the lane past Old Red Addie's grunting noise at her trough, squealing and whining for her already late breakfast, along the garden fence to the pignut trees, and into the middle of all the excitement.

To my absolute surprise, Shorty was using my stick and was trying to drive his cow around at Mom's orders. He was half crying. "Daddy'll lick me," he sobbed. "Don't let her die!"

Mom quickly took the trocar out of my hand, saying, "This is our last chance." I also heard her say under her breath, "Please help me do it," and I knew she wasn't talking to me.

Nobody knew how hard it was going to be for Mom to press that trocar against Babe's left flank, just about seven inches east of her left hipbone and, with a quick hard jab, thrust it in. But it was the only thing left to do. Even while Mom was swishing iodine on the trocar and on the spot she was going to shove the trocar into, I kept thinking, *Maybe if we save her, it'll be easier for Shorty's family to become Christians than if we don't.*

Poor Mom, my thoughts kept telling me. *This'll be one of the hardest things she ever had to do.* Mom always had such a tender heart and couldn't stand to see anything get hurt. Once when she had accidentally stepped on a little chicken and smashed it, she'd cried and had been sad for half the day.

I saw her face was set, and I knew she was making herself do it. "We saved Jersey Jill this way once when you were just a little boy, Bill," she said. "You wouldn't remember."

I didn't know where she'd gotten the cloth

to put the iodine on with, till I saw a torn place in her apron. It was one of her prettiest kitchen aprons, too, I remembered—and that was a silly thing to remember at a time like that.

And then I saw Mom's face go white as she took the trocar and measured the distance from the hipbone out to just the right place. "I'm—I'm—afraid I just can't do it." She gave me a helpless look. "Your father did it to Jersey Jill. Maybe you—"

Maybe me?

I cringed.

I hated to hurt anything, too, although I had operated on a snake once to try to save Warty, Dad's favorite toad, which we thought the snake had swallowed. If I was going to be a doctor someday, I might as well get a little experience on a cow. I might as well!

And I knew I had to act quick. Old Babe's knees were buckling. In a few more minutes she'd be dead. I knew it!

I let loose of the halter I'd been helping Guenther hold, took the trocar from Mom's hand, found the spot, and gripped the handle hard with both hands, knowing what a tough hide a cow had. I'd have to press the sharp point clear through. I hoped it wasn't too dull from the cured cowhide I'd pushed it through yesterday.

I tensed my biceps, which wouldn't be much help, because I had to push down rather than pull up. And then I jabbed! Hard!

9

There hadn't been anything in *What to Do Before the Doctor Arrives* to tell the average farmer what to expect one-sixteenth of a second after he has jabbed a triangular-pointed trocar through the tough cowhide of a live cow's left flank and into the paunch itself, which is not only full of ladino clover but is as tight as a dirigible full of gas.

I'd have been a little more careful to get out of the way *quick* if I had known that in a flash of a second there would be a noise like a train rushing past when you are standing a few feet from the tracks and a terrific roar of wind, which you not only hear but you feel, and it almost blows you over.

Also, there wasn't anything in the chapter I'd read that said an odor would come screaming out with the gas, worse than the smell of the worst polecat a boy ever caught in a trap, and an entirely different kind. And I wasn't prepared for what else came out.

I jumped back out of the way, smacking into Shorty and bowling him over. The two of us landed in the clover not far from where Mom herself was, holding her nose with her apron. It was the only thing handy to hold it with while quite a lot of that wild blue cow's breakfast, most of it being ladino clover, came roaring out as if it had been shot from a cannon and scattered itself all around everywhere.

For some reason, as I tried to untangle myself from Shorty—who was sobbing over his cow, thinking we had *really* killed her—I didn't even wonder if maybe she had accidentally eaten any *four-leafed* clovers. Most people like to pretend it means good luck to find one.

But the operation was what doctors call a complete success. At least, it was so far. After the first explosion, which was like a volcano erupting and spraying green lava all around, the noise settled down to a hissing sound like steam escaping from a threshing machine engine. There was a rumbling noise inside old Babe, and she began to get smaller. In only a little while, I noticed that her eyes weren't as bleary as they had been and she wasn't gasping for breath or heaving, and I knew we'd saved her life.

Mom knew it, too, and said so, which is how I was sure of it myself. "She'll act indifferent and just stand around for a few hours like she's lost all interest in life, and then, if she does like Jersey Jill did, she'll start eating again," Mom explained. "We're *so* glad she's going to be all right, Guenther," she said to Shorty. "It would have been a tragedy to lose such a fine cow. Blue is such a rare color. I think, when she gets over having lost her baby, she'll give lots more milk, too, and be more satisfied." Mom extended her hand, which I noticed was trembling, and stroked old Babe on the shoulder and patted her neck.

And Babe, hardly knowing she was alive yet, didn't act scared or jumpy but just stood still like a statue.

I don't know what happened in Shorty's mind while Mom was saying those kind words and stroking his blue cow. But all of a sudden I saw him look at her as if he thought she was wonderful. Then he looked all around as though he had thought of something else or was looking for something.

"What made her get that way?" he asked.

"The clover. She gorged herself with dew-wet clover, and that formed gas, and—"

All of a surprising sudden, Shorty's eyes focused on something away down at the foot of the hill in the clover field. Then he quickly dived for my ash stick that was lying a few feet away, grabbed it up, and, like a boy leaping into a race, was off on the fastest run I ever saw a boy his size start on.

He flew toward Jersey Jill, who was standing in knee-deep ladino clover with her head down, eating as if it was the best-tasting breakfast she had ever had and she didn't care what might happen to her.

"Come on!" Guenther yelled back to me over one of his shoulders.

And that's when I came to myself. I wasn't worried, though, because I'd fed Jersey Jill some bran shorts and some dry alfalfa, which she'd been eating while I milked her. And besides, there wasn't nearly as much dew on the clover she was eating as there had been on that with which Babe had stuffed *her* stomach a while ago. The sun was up high now and shining on everything. It was going to be a very wonderful day.

I left Mom and Shorty's cow standing there and ran through the clover toward Jersey Jill. After all, I didn't want Dad to come home and find so much excitement going on around the place when I was supposed to be the man of the house and of the barn and look after things.

But Shorty was serious. He'd seen what too much clover had done to *his* cow, and Mom had told him why, and he was going to save *my* cow by driving her out of the field. He was quite a ways ahead of me when I stopped and looked back at Mom to see what she thought, but I couldn't see her face well enough to tell.

Shorty's excited voice came up the hill to where I was as he cried out to Jersey Jill, "Get out of here! Don't you know that stuff'll kill you?"

A lump came into my throat, and I couldn't see straight for a second. That boy who had caused us so much trouble for weeks and weeks, and who had hated me most of the time clear up to a half hour ago, might turn into a good boy yet.

I hurried after him to help him drive Jersey Jill back up to the gate and out, and also so that he wouldn't seem like such a dumbbell for not knowing she wasn't in any such danger as his cow had been—eating all that clover on an empty stomach.

I was thinking about who had *really* saved his cow, and it wasn't any red-haired, freckle-faced boy. It was somebody's wonderful mother, who had had presence of mind enough to know what to do and had done it.

That round-and-round note Dad had written on the egg and left in the basket had told the truth.

Jersey Jill didn't like the ash stick Shorty was using on her, so she let herself be driven back to the gate at the pignut trees, where to my surprise I noticed Babe standing alone. Mom was gone.

I looked all around, wondering, *Where on earth?*

Then I saw her blue dress and her kind of windblown gray brown hair as she ran past the henhouse and the chicken coops by the orchard fence and on past the kitchen door. I heard her calling to somebody, and right away I saw a flash of something yellow about three feet high out by the walnut tree. It was Charlotte Ann, my little sister, in her cute little yellow dress, going through the open front gate and out onto the road.

Open gate! I saw it and at the same time wondered, *How come?* I turned quickly to Shorty and asked, "You leave the gate open when you came through?"

He saw what I saw, and he answered, "It was already open."

A sickening sensation came over me as I realized that there was only one way it could have been left open. Theodore Collins's only boy, who had gone through it last night to go to see what had made the noise at old Babe's corral, had neglected to shut it when he came back. That made two gates he had left open—not a very good record. I sighed heavily. Then I heard Babe breathing—still a little bit noisily—beside me, and I felt better, knowing she was going to live.

Just then I saw Mom catch up with Charlotte Ann, sweep her up into her arms, and start back through the gate and toward the house.

I guess Shorty saw them coming, too, because he said, "You have an awful nice mother."

I remembered the phone conversation I'd had with *his* mother quite a few weeks ago, and I answered, "Your mother's awful nice, too."

Shorty still had my ash stick, and when I finished saying that, he did what boys nearly always do with sticks when they carry them. He took a swipe at the first thing he saw that was close by, which was a tall stalk of wild lettuce growing by the gatepost. He hit it so hard he knocked off three or four of its yellow-rayed flowers, leaving that many milky-juiced broken stems on which the flowers had been growing.

I didn't find out till later that Charlotte Ann was another reason Mom had been a little slow in getting up to the pignut trees with her bottle of drenching medicine. She'd had to put Charlotte Ann into her own picket fence corral beside the house, so she wouldn't follow her and get in our way and get hurt. And Charlotte Ann had managed to get out and through the open gate.

About fifteen minutes later, when we didn't need him, the veterinarian came, and we told him the story of what we had done.

"Who used the trocar?" he asked, looking from one to the other of us.

Shorty spoke up, saying, "*He* did," motioning to me. "He saved my cow's life."

"You the doctor?" The vet looked at me the way Dad does sometimes when he especially likes me.

I felt myself feeling proud of myself. Not wanting anybody to see me grinning, which I could tell I was starting to do, I quickly said, looking at Mom, "I had a wonderful nurse."

The vet himself grinned then and chuckled as he gave Mom a friendly look. He turned next to Shorty, who was snapping a rope onto Babe's halter—Babe was beginning to act a little more as though she knew she was alive and was glad of it—and said to him, "And what did you do?"

A mischievous expression galloped across Guenther's face as he answered, "I furnished the patient."

Then I got another surprise. As you know, Poetry had never seen a *purple* cow. Well, I had never seen a *blue* one before, and it had been hard for me to accept Shorty's quadruped as belonging to the cattle family. She was so wild and so just the opposite from Jersey Jill. But when the vet finished what he said next, I looked with real admiration in my mind at the four-footed animal I had just operated on.

This is what the doctor said to Shorty: "The Milking Shorthorn is one of the specially developed breeds. To have one of them be blue—and such a *deep* blue—is *something!* But it does happen once in a while."

Mom spoke up then. "She lost her calf a month or so ago in a car accident, and she's been a little nervous ever since. I understand the calf died right in front of her eyes. She'll get over it in time, but it must have upset her terribly. She is a beauty, isn't she?"

I looked at Babe's very deep blue color, which she was nearly all over, and at the almost snow-white underpart of her, and for some reason she wasn't nearly as bad-looking as she had been when we'd first seen her down at the mouth of the branch.

Shorty looked at his cow, too, when Mom said that about her, and his eyes lit up. Then he explained to all of us—and maybe to the veterinarian especially, "She didn't have very good pasture where we lived before. That's why she's kind of skinny. But she's been picking up a little since she came here."

The vet, who was getting his doctor's case ready to put into his car, stopped and looked Babe over again. He said to Shorty, "She picked up a little too *much* this morning and got *too* fat for a while. Well, I've another case waiting for me over across the creek—bad case of actinomycosis!"

He was just getting into his car, when Shorty asked, "What's actino—what kind of trouble is that?"

"Just a lumpy jaw," the vet answered.

He was slamming his car door when Shorty called after him, "Is there a special name for what my cow had?"

"The bloat?" the doctor said. "Sure. Your Milking Shorthorn had a bad case of tympanites!"

I looked at Guenther's face, and he was as proud as anything—not only of his cow because she was a special breed but because she had had such an important-sounding sickness.

"Tympanites," he repeated to himself and acted like a much smaller boy with a new toy, not even thinking to say good-bye to the doctor as he drove away.

About two hours later, when Dad came driving up to our mailbox, Charlotte Ann was in her picket fence corral by the plum tree, playing with her dolls. I was out in the garden hoeing potatoes, not even bothering to save the nice-looking fishing worms I kept accidentally digging up. Every gate on the farm was absolutely and for sure closed and absolutely and for sure carefully latched, and my heart was pounding for wondering what he would say when he found out all the exciting things that had happened.

Old Babe, out in her own pasture again, was munching away on some bluegrass not far from the path that leads down to the spring. The hole in the fence, where she had broken through before she'd come through our two gates, had been fixed by Bill Collins himself, who had learned how to build fences earlier in the spring. Shorty Long had helped a little.

There wasn't a thing around the farm that was wrong that I could think of—except the way I felt about what *had* been wrong earlier in the morning.

I wondered how soon Dad would find out about everything, and who would start to tell him first—Mom or I—and what would he say first.

One minute after he was out of the car and had whisked up Charlotte Ann into his arms and was carrying her toward the house, he stopped and picked up something that had been lying beside Mom's tulip bed. "What's the *trocar* doing, lying out here in the weather?"

And that's how the thing started. The same boy who had forgotten to shut two gates had also forgotten to put the trocar back into the cabinet.

Mom had seen and heard the car drive in, too, and was outdoors just in time to hear the question and to start to answer it.

My heart was still pounding, and I felt worried inside. I certainly hadn't been very much of a man of the house, I thought sadly, wondering what Mom would say. A lot would depend on her.

We were at the dinner table before I was sure everybody was going to be forgiven by each other and everything would be all right again. Dad had just prayed, when Mom said in a serious voice, "I don't know what I'd do if I couldn't pray anytime and wherever I am."

Dad's gray green eyes looked at her from under his shaggy-ledged brows, and he answered, "You're a wonderful wife and mother."

When he said that, her face kind of lit up, and she said, "You've said that before in a roundabout way."

I saw their four eyes meet for a few seconds, and it seemed I wasn't going to have to worry about whether I was a wonderful boy and son or not. In my mind's eye, I was in our dark kitchen shining my flashlight into a basket of eggs.

Suddenly I felt kind of brave and asked, "When do I get punished for being so forgetful about the gates?"

The answer was certainly a pleasant surprise. Dad asked, "How do you feel inside about it?"

I had hardly eaten a bite yet, but just then I had a bite of bread and butter that needed to be chewed a little more before I could answer. When I could get a word out, I said, "Not very good."

Dad looked at me for quite a while, not chewing or saying a thing. Then he said, "I'm proud of you, son. You're all right." And he changed the subject, saying, "The bass season opens next week."

Just like that, the heavy load that was inside of me somewhere wasn't anymore there than a dragonfly is when you see it perched on your bobber out in the water, and you get a bite and your bobber twitches a little, and the dragonfly's wings swish it to some other place quicker than a flash.

"We'll cut the clover tomorrow, put the hay up as soon as it's dry, and away we'll go—you, Leslie Thompson's father and his son, and Mrs. Theodore Collins's husband—just for fun. Want to go? Want to make a try for that bear we talked about last month?"

"He killed a big one this morning," Mom said.

I was making short work of a bite of steak right then, so I didn't answer till I could talk and be understood. "I pretty near killed an innocent cow, if that's what you mean," I answered.

"It's not what I mean. What I mean is that you don't hate Guenther Long anymore. Isn't that right?"

I frowned into my plate, thinking. And while I was looking down, I absentmindedly shut my right eye, looked down the left side of my nose to see if I could see any fuzz on my stuck-out upper lip, and couldn't. The fact is, I had *enjoyed* helping Shorty fix the pasture fence where old Babe had broken through.

Then I remembered what his mother had said over the telephone, and I answered Mom: "That's why his folks moved back to Sugar

Creek, so he'd have some Christian boys to play with."

Just then the phone rang our ring. They let me go answer it, and it was good old Poetry. He had heard in some roundabout way about the fishing trip. "Just think," his squawky voice said cheerfully, "we're going away up North, clear up where Paul Bunyan and his blue cow used to live a long time ago!"

"I'm going to kill a bear when we get there," I said. "*A real* one."

When I hung up to go back to finish one of the best dinners I had ever had, I was feeling wonderful inside—absolutely wonderful.

One of the positively first things I'll do when we get back from that bass fishing trip— if I can find time between doing chores and making garden and milking cows and other farmwork—is to tell you all about it in another north woods story.

I certainly hope I'll have time. I also hope I'll manage to bring back a big black bearskin for our living-room floor.

Moody Press, a ministry of the Moody Bible Institute, is designed for education, evangelization, and edification. If we may assist you in knowing more about Christ and the Christian life, please write us without obligation: Moody Press, c/o MLM, Chicago, Illinois 60610.